THE VINYL FRONTIER

LESSONS LEARNED
BOOK 4

LOLA WEST

WWW.SMARTYPANTSROMANCE.COM

COPYRIGHT

CHAPTER ONE

ZACK

"DICK'S HERE!" boomed Richard "Dickie" Bartholomew Matthews as a handful of my fraternity brothers and I clambered through the doors of the campus community center.

Dickie lived up to his namesake. He really was a dick. He was blond and about six feet tall, wearing rumpled khaki chinos, an orange polo and brown leather docksiders. There was no boating adventure planned, but good ol' Dickie was notoriously prepared for an impromptu sailing spree. Best case scenario, he was ready to captain a friggin' frigate. Worst case, he wore ratty old inappropriate shoes everywhere, all the time.

I had the pleasure of Dickie's company each and every day. He was a member of Sigma Tau Omega, a legacy brother, like me, so I pretended to like him. Honestly, I pretended to like most of my brothers. I drank beer from tapped kegs with them, listened to them talk smack about women they thought were hot, and knew, at any given meal, I could be eating from a plate covered in their germs. They all looked like they literally pulled their clothes from a dirty laundry hamper.

But Dickie was a particularly slovenly person and a moron to boot. I truly disliked him. And yet, like a starched marionette, tethered to my father's wishes, I lifted a smile at Dickie's dickish joke, maintaining my cover as the affable ruler of these circus buffoons.

When it came right down to it, that was my lot: king of those who thought themselves Spartans, the entitled soon-to-be rulers of other men born in less fortunate circumstances. My job was to wrangle them, to present myself as their squeaky-clean front man, a civilized human head on the writhing body of a pig. According to my father, who, with an air of pomp and circumstance, regularly referred to himself as a senior senator in the U.S. Congress, fraternity brothers were the foundational relationships that catapulted a political career.

Admittedly, boarding school buddies also contributed to this mythical foundation, which I was pretty sure was just a fancy way to say guys with bottomless checkbooks. But you could never be a hundred percent certain because my father often repeated himself. He talked in circles, hoping I wouldn't notice his duplicitous nature or the ever-expanding guidelines dictating who and what was acceptable for a son of political royalty. I noticed, but I didn't buck. Nowhere to go.

As usual, lost and uninformed, Dickie turned to me and asked, "Where is this snooze fest, Prez?" I was the president of our fraternity, but I hated that he called me Prez with a Z.

"Downstairs," I answered curtly. I didn't talk much, and when I did, I often chose brevity. Being concise kept people from misconstruing your words. I crossed in front of Dickie and pressed the elevator button on the wall.

Dickie pretended to hump said wall and boasted, "Aww-yeah, we going downstairs, boys." He made all things into sexual jokes.

Inside was a touch warmer than it had been outside, so I unbuttoned the sleeves of my freshly laundered white oxford and focused on neatly rolling up the cuffs rather than rolling my eyes at Dickie's juvenile lewdness.

Another winner, Andrew Hurston, laughed at Dickie's seriously unfunny behavior. "That your plan tonight, dickface? You gonna get some unaffiliated ass?"

Jesus, it better not be. We were in the campus center because, right before Christmas break, these morons had almost gotten our fraternity put on probation. They'd built a homemade waterslide out a second-story window that ran off into a three-foot-deep blow-up pool. It was not only cold. It was downright dangerous. Someone literally could have died. Luckily, I was a smooth talker, so instead of going before the IFC, I spent my Christmas break campaigning on our behalf and got us a sweetheart of a deal: a few community service outings and mandatory attendance and sponsorship of a number of non-fraternity events hosted by the student government.

Tonight's event was a particularly wily one for this crew: a dry, silent disco to celebrate the start of the spring semester. Or, rather, the antithesis of what my fraternity brothers defined as enjoyment, which for them meant raging, loud, packed hump fests, doused in alcohol and other assorted sundries.

Dickie ceased the gyration of his hips and smirked at Andrew. "Unaffiliated or not, if the hunnies come a-knocking …" He trailed off.

What did that even mean? Like, when we pledged our fraternity, did we sign some unspoken agreement that we would only date girls in sororities? Or was it just human nature to draw us-and-them lines so we could take sides? Also, what "hunny," or any quality woman, would be interested in someone who smelled like dirty socks?

As the elevator bell went ding, I found myself wishing I was Harry Potter or maybe Luke Skywalker or the ever-so-elegant Captain Jean-Luc Picard. Basically, any hero with the moral fiber to stand up to the injustice of common-place assholiness without worrying about the social consequences. Because I wanted to tell Richard "Dickie" Bartholomew Matthews to stop being such a fucking idiot, but I couldn't. I was one of them—a Death Eater—and when you live on the dark side, your people can turn on you for even the slightest infraction.

I held back the elevator door and watched them pile in before taking my position at the helm. I spoke calmly as I said, "Remember, we are here cleaning up a mess. Be on your best behavior and schmooze, but make sure not to insult anyone."

Andrew asked, "How long do we have to stay?"

"An hour, maybe less," I replied.

Ashton Vos, who was from Texas and vaguely reminiscent of someone worth talking to, said, "We can't fuck this up, y'all. Zack did us a mighty favor getting us this deal."

"All praise the Prez," Dickie chanted like he was breaking a huddle as the elevator doors opened. My motley crew piled out, and we headed through the set of glass doors in front of us, which led to the main event area of the campus center.

The student government had transformed the space so it looked like a dance club—albeit a slightly cheesy one. Mostly, they'd made it dark and set up a lot of spinning colored lights. There was a dance floor in the center, surrounded by the cafe tables that were always there. Off to my left was a DJ and a guy handing out headphones. For those of us living the college life, it was still early, only ten on a Saturday night, so the dance floor wasn't particularly hopping yet.

I turned to my brothers. "Go grab headphones and make fools of yourselves.

I want them to remember we were here." As they started to move, I said, "Wait," and their faces turned back to mine, "no humping anyone."

Dickie smirked. "Damn, Prez, you ruin all the fun."

I shook my head at him, and then they were off. I casually headed to the corner of the room where Dr. Ford, the Dean of Arts and Sciences, was standing. Best to say hello. Dr. Ford was my favorite kind of people: matter of fact, to the point and unusually intelligent.

She nodded at me as I approached. "Mr. Worthington."

"Dr. Ford." I nodded back but also offered my hand for her to shake. She shook hands like she owned the earth. I envied the technique and shook hands with her any chance I got, trying to commit the feeling to memory.

"I see you've brought your team."

"Yes, my brothers are happy to be here, ma'am." I looked out at the dance floor as we spoke. Andrew was doing the sprinkler, and Dickie was circling him doing the shopping cart. For once, they were behaving exactly as I wished.

"I bet." She seeded the words with undertones of a scoff, but she didn't actually scoff.

I added, "They will also happily help with the cleanup tomorrow."

"Yes, I imagine they will." She turned to me, her voice softer than usual. "It was impressive what you did at that hearing last week, convincing the honor board this punishment was fitting, when you and I both know social probation was the fitting punishment." She wasn't looking for a response, so I didn't give her one. She continued, "You rule with a heavy hand, don't you, Zack?"

"As the situation demands," I answered honestly, shifting my weight to an at-ease military stance, feet shoulder-width apart and my hands clasped behind my back. I hadn't served, but I was in ROTC, and depending on my law school applications, the military was still a possibility for me.

She asked, "You ever, I don't know, act like a kid?"

I wasn't offended. Many people found my maturity off-putting. "I am not a kid, Dr. Ford. I'm twenty years old. Legally an adult in pretty much all countries and all states—although still a minor in Puerto Rico for one more year."

She looked at me quizzically. "Huh, that true?"

"Yes, ma'am."

"Well, either way, maybe you should get out there and dance a little. I think letting loose might do you good."

Time to go. "I'll take it under advisement." I smiled, a big, gentle, open smile I practiced in the mirror. It was my smile that made people think I trusted them.

"I'm going to wander about and say my hellos. Always nice to see you, ma'am." I offered my hand a second time, eager for her shake. As I walked away, I could still feel the force of it.

There was a snack bar across the room, so I headed there, ordered myself a soda and then meandered about the room until I came to a stop a bit of a distance from the guy managing the headphones. I had no intention of dancing. I was there to observe, supervise, and make sure my brothers behaved themselves.

Leaning against the wall, I nursed my soda and watched the growing crowd. The event seemed to be somewhat of a success. And it was sort of magical to watch people dance in utter silence. Even though they heard music, the fact that you couldn't hear it completely reframed their movements. Strangely, dancers without music were akin to astronauts without gravity—floating in a way that felt impossible to understand.

I glanced at my watch, noticing we were closing in on the hour I'd promised, and I was considering rounding up my crew when she walked in and took my breath away. She was a little pixie of a thing, five feet at most. Her hair was dark, and there was tons of it, long and silky, and in an enticing disarray. She also had huge eyes, giant slightly buggy saucers she outlined in thick, dark liner. She wasn't curvy or busty. She wasn't classically pretty in any way, but something about her was utterly magnetic. She reminded me of Arwen from *Lord of the Rings*, downright ethereal.

She strolled with purpose to the headphone guy, pointed to a pair, silently questioning if she was free to just take them. He nodded, smiling at her in a way that made me uniquely unhappy. I didn't often find myself concerned with the way strange men flirted with a woman I'd never met, and, honestly, I was sort of shocked by my reaction. I even cleared my throat like I had something to say. To whom, I am not exactly sure, but watching him talk to her made me want to rant at someone.

The only thing keeping my irrational response in check was her total indifference. At first, she seemed to listen with great intensity as he pointed to the parts and explained the headphones, watching his mouth as he spoke, but when he handed them to her, she gave him a tight smile, tipped her head in thanks, and immediately walked away without having said anything.

I watched her back as she approached the dance floor. She was wearing jeans, a black band T-shirt and black Converse. Her overall look was plain but also punky. Once she picked her spot, she half-faced me again, and then grasped the headphones between her thighs as she twisted her hair into a messy bun at the nape of her neck. Hair fixed, she fussed with the headphones for a bit before putting them on, instantly becoming a punky Princess Leia.

I was into her, drawn to her in a way that didn't make sense. She wasn't part of the plan. I was one hundred percent sure my father, senior senator in the U.S. Congress, would not approve. This was not the kind of girl who stood next to you on the podium as you swore to uphold the law. This was the kind of girl who went with you to the county fair, screamed something profane from the top of the Ferris wheel, and licked the cotton candy off her fingers.

She looked like normal and wild all rolled into one. I bet she hung out in her dorm room with friends eating junk food and wearing pajamas. Her life was regular, the kind of life where you borrowed your parents' car to run to the store and decorated your childhood bedroom with posters of your favorite bands. I was not this kind of person, not at all.

Tranced out watching her, I didn't hear Ashton next to me until he said, "Huh, I never would have thought punky was your type."

"She's not," I said, my voice calm and completely even. Luckily, I was not easy to fluster.

"Say what you will, but I've known you three years, Zack, and I've never seen you watch a woman the way you were just watching that one."

In my head, Yoda said, *Observant, this one was. Give him something, you must.*

"I admit, she's interesting to look at. Unique in some way, but not for me. I am not interested in the way you're implying."

"Of course not," he said, his voice laced with sarcasm. "You have a plan."

I nodded. I did. It wasn't my plan per se, but I followed it.

"You should go dance with her," Ashton suggested.

For a second I considered it, sauntering up, smiling at her, offering a voiceless hello (because headphones), getting her silent confirmation that I was free to dance in her airspace, maybe some soundless giggles at my foolish dance moves. My chest tightened at the thought of the imaginary interaction, and I had to take a deep breath to right myself.

"Don't be silly," I said, but there was a whisper in my tone that gave away the longing I felt.

Ashton tilted to the left with curiosity. "Actually, I was thinking you should trust me to round up and lord over our brothers for the next hour."

Confused by his offer, I asked, "What do you mean?"

"I saw you talking to Dr. Ford and thought it might be good if you stayed behind, made it look like you cared about this event, above and beyond the fraternity's obligation…"

I narrowed my eyes at him. What was he doing?

"…You know, to make a good impression." He wasn't looking at me anymore, and it was clear he had an ulterior motive.

"I think she knows I am dedicated. Not to worry."

He sighed, clearly frustrated. Then, he dropped his voice to an almost inaudible tone. "I was also thinking, once we were gone, you could ignore the plan for like five minutes. It's much easier to break rules when no one's watching."

Yes, but not when someone knew your intentions.

"Thank you for your concern, Vos, but I'm good." I thought of him as Ashton, but we all called him by his last name. I pushed off the wall I was leaning on. "What you can do is tell the guys to pack it up. I'm just going to say my goodbyes."

"Sir, yes, sir," he teased, saluting me.

I volleyed a little laugh in his direction, and, as I walked away, I mumbled, "Douche canoe." I was only loud enough for him and me to hear. And he seemed to appreciate my quip because I heard him laughing in my wake.

As I made my way through the room saying my goodbyes to the key members of the student government, I couldn't help but continue to notice her. She had her eyes closed and was holding the headphones, cradling them to her ears, concentrating on the music and swaying her body. She wasn't dancing per se, more like vibing to the sounds. Beyond her T-shirt, her passion for music seemed obvious to me. She wasn't at this event to dance and be silly. She was here to listen. I circled the room slowly, savoring my last glimpses of her.

Eventually, I got to Dr. Ford, who said, "Mr. Worthington, I'm surprised you're still here."

"On my way out, ma'am." I smiled. "Just saying my goodbyes."

She pointed up toward the glass doors we had entered through. "Yes, but isn't that your crew getting in the elevator?"

I looked in the direction she was pointing, just in time to see the gleeful look on Ashton's face as he herded our brothers into the elevator. *Sneaky bastard.*

"It is. I just wanted to check that you didn't need anything."

"No, I think we can manage without your assistance," she snickered. "But I appreciate the offer."

A shade embarrassed but still poised, I shrugged. "Alrighty then, I'm gonna head out."

"Or you could take my original suggestion and dance."

I held out my hand for a third time in one evening. "Have a good night, ma'am."

I had no intention of dancing, none. But instead of shaking my hand, Dr. Ford handed me a pair of headphones. "You can use mine. They're clean. I promise I don't have germs."

Damnit. "Perhaps for one song." I smiled tightly at her.

"Or two," she offered.

My smile still stiff, I turned to the dance floor and put on the headphones. When it came to dancing, I was pretty much daft, unless it was ballroom, of course. My parents had made sure I was proficient in terms of the foxtrot and the waltz, but having fun and going freestyle on the dance floor was not in my wheelhouse. After pressing the channel button on the side, I eventually landed on Chubby Checker's "The Twist." I could handle that. It had prescribed movements, and I knew what they were.

I crossed onto the dance floor, far enough that I blended into the crowd and got a bit closer to my punky pixie. I absolutely wasn't going to dance with her, but I thought I could mitigate the suffering associated with this trial by having her in my line of sight. Reluctantly, I began to twist. At first, I felt ridiculous, like everyone was watching and judging, but after a few moments, I started to take in the joy on the faces around me, and my anxiety abated. Surrounded by all the others dancing to whatever beats they could hear, I felt camaraderie. We were a ragtag group of oddballs, jiggling our limbs this way and that, and yet, it didn't feel foolish—it felt inspired.

When "The Twist" ended, it was replaced by Whitney Houston cooing "I Wanna Dance with Somebody," and just like that, I lost sight of the plan.

I shifted through the crowd, milling this way and that, until I was standing just in front of her. As if she sensed my presence, she opened her eyes. I had this hound dog stuffed animal when I was a kid. Its eyes were massive, way too big for its face. She reminded me of it. Something about its disproportionate glance was irresistible.

She studied me politely. I smiled, not a practiced one, just the natural elation that was coursing through my body. She smiled back, and I started to dance.

I was sure I was terrible, but she seemed to love it. I even mouthed the lyrics. She laughed and mouthed, "Whitney Houston?"

I nodded and popped my eyebrows, silently saying, *oh yeah, I'm rockin' out to Whitney.*

She gave me a thumbs-up. And then she started to dance with me, following my lead. We shimmied and shook. We wiggled and waggled. We tweaked and twerked. We made faces, and sang lyrics and played air guitar. We were unhinged and silly together, and it was genuinely fun. More fun than I remembered having, ever.

I had no idea how much time had passed, but eventually a tall girl with frizzy blonde curls came up behind her and tapped her on the shoulder. When she turned to respond, I stopped moving, as if my newfound ability to dance with reckless abandon hindered on her gaze. Suddenly still, I became aware that my breathing was labored and my heart was pounding from exertion.

I slid off my headphones, letting them wrap around my neck. Only then did I realize she was still wearing hers. My ears free, I could hear the blonde girl speaking to her.

Blondie said, "We're leaving if you still want a ride."

With her headphones on, my punky pixie wasn't hearing her words. Instead, she focused on her friend's hands moving quickly in front of her. They were speaking in American Sign Language.

She turned back to me. Smiling, she signed, "Thank you."

I took sign language as an elective in my junior year of high school. I'd thought it would be an easy "A" and look interesting on my college applications, but it was actually quite demanding, and ultimately I was irritated that I took it.

Her friend interpreted for her. "She said thank you."

I looked to her friend and then back to her. I was totally confused. Why was she signing? She wasn't deaf. She couldn't be. We were just listening to music.

"I know," I said tentatively and then looked at her friend again. "Why is she signing?"

The blonde girl rolled her eyes. "Because that's how she communicates. Duh."

Shocked, I looked back at my punky pixie, just in time to watch the smile I'd delighted in slip away.

CHAPTER TWO

MOLLY

WITH FORCE and using only my shoulder, I pushed open the door to my dorm and braved the cold. As usual, my hands were otherwise disposed, always, always tapping out rhythms with my drumsticks. Managing the weight of my backpack and the door required some finesse because the wind pushed back, pressing the door shut, so I heaved my body into it, still absolutely unwilling to pocket my sticks.

New England in late January was just frickin' gray. The vistas were barren, stark trees, stone buildings, hazy skyscape, and if there wasn't an actual endless sea of snow, then the ground was spotted with dirty, stained, melting plops of used-to-be snow. Not gonna lie. Not my favorite environment. I grew up in Florida's endless months of sunshine, so winter was particularly oppressive for me.

But still I forged ahead. Sometimes it seemed like human persistence and determination were part of the northeast's landscape. Like the energy left behind by the centuries of people who managed to survive the harsh environment without the modern convenience of electric heat and stoves informed the resilience of the contemporary inhabitants, like it was their job to bear the brunt of the brutal winter because the early settlers and the Native Americans certainly had it worse.

Managing to beat out the wind, I headed for the little coffee kiosk on the quad. I wanted to quickly grab something warm and cozy before making my way across campus to day one of Research Methods with Dr. Victor Hanover. I'd love to say the first day of classes sounded thrilling, but, honestly, I wasn't even the slightest bit excited. Day one of any class when you are deaf and require accommodations is nerve-racking. Sadly, it almost never goes smoothly.

People like to think that with modern student resource centers, people with disabilities now have super convenient access to any and all things but, um, not so much. That level of comfort, showing up to class and just having everything fall into place, that is an ableist daydream. And on top of that, the scuttlebutt was that Dr. Hanover didn't suffer fools, so, yeah, I was just generally tense, like a legit head-to-toe stress ball situation. Hence, the stop at the kiosk for the sweet, sweet relief of an overly creamy and sugary caffeinated beverage. Sure, I fully understood that caffeine and stress weren't really besties, but sometimes you have to throw caution to the wind.

So, I was cold, strolling, casually meandering toward my destination, while busting out air rhythms with my drumsticks and trying not to think about the guy who danced with me at the silent disco. Our little groove fest was almost seventy-two hours in the past, and I knew I should just forget the whole thing altogether. I saw the look he gave me when he realized I was deaf. I knew he was surprised and confused, and the tightness of his brow screamed not delighted.

But there was something about my moments with him that I just couldn't seem to shake off. It wasn't necessarily a connection, but it was something. It was something about the way he looked at me. A certain glimmer in his eyes that started a little fire under my sternum. Okay, maybe it was also something about the way he looked.

At first glance, he wasn't what I usually gravitated toward. I liked a wilder-looking man. Someone whose exterior presentation seemed like they might get what it feels like to be different. Generally, the men I dated had green hair and gauges, or a wallet chain and an irreverent T-shirt. Also, they were always Deaf.

I actively chose to date other deaf people because I didn't want to be with someone who underestimated me. I didn't want a guy who laughed at or questioned my desire to be a professional drummer. And while most deaf people thought I was overreaching, hearing folks looked at me with a weird combination of *how is that possible?* and *well, isn't that cute*. It was a facial expression that could make pretty much anyone lose their lunch. So, I figured when it came to dating, best stick to my kind. It worked for me.

And, honestly, it worked for my Deaf parents, who were already peeved at me for not attending a university that catered to deaf students. As far as they were concerned, Deaf universities were like Deaf utopias, and they couldn't seem to understand why I would miss out on that opportunity. Just to be clear: deaf universities don't generally have highly sought-after music departments, but try explaining that to them. They loved me, and I loved them, but exhausting.

Anyway, the guy at the silent disco wasn't artsy, and he wasn't deaf, but he was sort of unforgettable. He looked like an off-duty Marine, real clean-cut and typical. He was tall and lean, well kept, proper and visibly pompous. But when he was dancing with me, that look changed. Suddenly, he was loose. He had a wild rhythm, a sparkle beneath his skin. Watching him shake his moneymaker, I became distinctly aware that he was beautiful. He was fit, with strong muscular shoulders and big man hands, but he was also alive, vibrant, kind of kooky and odd in a way that made me feel like grinning.

And I found that, thinking of him, I was still grinning, totally forgetting the cold, while I strolled across campus toward my caffeinated cup of comfort. It was a vicious cycle, really. For a few moments, I'd get lost in the memories of our silliness together and glow on the inside, and then, boom, I'd remember the rest, those moments when he realized I was deaf and clearly didn't like it. Suddenly, I'd feel the snap of his distaste, the sour in his gaze, and I'd have to remind myself that mooning over a jerky frat boy wasn't my MO. It wasn't my job to teach people to be open, accepting and accommodating. It was their job to be frickin' decent people in the first place.

As I approached the kiosk, I gave myself just a little slack. There wasn't a ton of harm in savoring a moment with a stranger you'd most likely never connect with again. We didn't attend the world's largest college, but I was pretty sure my corner of our microcosm didn't have anything to do with his corner.

I'd been coming to the kiosk since my first semester, and it was pretty much manned by the same employees. Routines—things like being a repeat customer —made my interactions with the hearing world easier. So, as I approached the counter, I looked for a face I recognized, but no such luck. It should have occurred to me that, with the change of the semester, there would be new employees and schedules, etc. For a split second, I closed my eyes, really let the lids go heavy, and took a deep breath. Then, I shoved my drumsticks into the back pocket of my jeans and took out my phone.

Smartphones changed everything. I mean, yes, they changed the way the world works. They changed the movie and music industry and the ability to experience utter anonymity. They changed how our memory works and how we experience a moment. But all of that aside, they gave me a voice. I can literally type out what I need, and my phone will tell a hearing stranger how to help me.

It could also capture their response so I could understand their reply, although it wasn't always accurate. Still, genius level stuff right there.

The woman behind the counter was a little older, probably in her forties. She was already talking to me, her lips moving so quickly that I couldn't decipher the words, but I assumed it was something rote like, "How can I help you?" I looked her in the eye, making sure I had her full attention, then I held up my hand and lifted one finger, signaling for her to wait a second while I quickly typed out, "I am deaf" and hit the play button.

I watched her as my phone communicated for me. Right before she heard my words, there was a stitch of annoyance across her brow. Sometimes when I asked a person to wait a second, they thought I was finishing a text or something equally inconsiderate rather than communicating with them. I didn't really understand the pace of the hearing world, but I was one hundred percent certain my needs altered the pattern of communication, and that was a struggle for some. Not this lady though. As soon as the recording completed, she smiled and gave me a vigorous nod.

I typed, "Please may I have a giant salted caramel latte?" and then the charades began. First, she held up all the different cup sizes, trying to gather which one qualified as giant to me. Never mind that there was an actual size giant. It was a twenty-four-ounce cup. The kiosk sizes were small, medium, large and GIANT, sigh. Then she pointed to all the milks. Just milk please.

Then, the coffee. Decaf or regular? She was being kind. She didn't want to misinterpret me. But still, it was frustrating. I was one hundred and ten percent certain that if a hearing person ordered a giant salted caramel latte, they would just get one handed to them without the rigmarole. Trying not to get bitchy, I forced a smile and waited patiently for her to complete the process.

The line behind me was growing, and the pressure of other people waiting was giving me anxiety. It was that making-a-left-turn-across-lanes-of-traffic feeling. The roll in your stomach you feel when the cars are lining up behind you, but you just can't tell if the break in the oncoming vehicles is significant enough for you to safely make the turn.

Cup in hand and all marked up, she looked at me again, her brows pinched together in frustration. There was nothing for her to point to this time, but I knew what she needed: my name. I typed "Molly" and hit play. Relief flooded her features, and she smiled brightly as she scrawled the letters on the cup. I just prayed she didn't ask if I wanted a muffin.

The coffee took longer than I expected, so I raced to class, sure my interpreter would be waiting for me because that was what they usually did. They kinda lingered by the door or off to the side, shifting their weight, patiently biding their time until their job began. Obviously, if you got there first, you sat tight and awaited their arrival. That way, you went inside together and approached the professor to remind him that I was in his class and required certain accommodations.

But there was literally no one outside the door. I glanced at my watch. Class was supposed to start in three minutes. The interpreter should have been there.

Classrooms were one of the places where the new fandangled apps and smartphone magic tricks just didn't cut it. Classrooms were not a simple exchange of sentences. Learning is more complicated than that. It requires engagement on a different level. I couldn't just understand what a person says. I had to actually get it and be able to apply it myself. So, with my smartphone, could I get by without an interpreter in a class? Maybe, if I could somehow decipher all the typos dictation left behind. But would I be able to excel? Absolutely not.

I pulled out my phone and scrolled back through my emails to confirm my interpreter was meeting me. I'd already looked at the email from the learning center earlier in the morning because I wanted to see if it included the interpreter's name, but it only said "to be determined." I quickly read through the fine print, trying to see if there was someone to reach out to if my interpreter didn't show, but no such luck. My mouth felt pasty, the sugary claw of my coffee hanging on my teeth.

I looked left down the hall and then right—no one. No harried, frazzled, running-late interpreter to be found. Fuck, I was gonna have to go it alone.

Swallowing down my discomfort, I pulled open the door and entered the classroom. It was a big auditorium-style space with stepped rows of long desks and chairs. Most of the students were already in their seats. I felt their eyes on me as I crossed the room and headed for the man I assumed was Dr. Hanover. He was tall and fit with shaggy brown hair, but his clothes hung on him like they were at least a size or two too big. Still, he was handsome enough that interacting with him felt doubly intimidating. But I had to. Somehow, I had to communicate my situation. If I just took my seat, there was no way I would possibly understand what was happening in the class.

I approached the desk, and he didn't look up. I was pretty sure I'd made some noise. I had a general awareness that noise was all around me, that people made noise all the time, even if I didn't hear it. As a deaf person, sneaking up on someone silently was not really a thing. Still, Dr. Hanover kept his eyes locked on what looked like a gradebook that was lying on the desk between us. It was possible he was speaking and that he knew I was there, but unless I crouched down and looked up from beneath him so I could see his lips, I wouldn't be able to tell what was happening.

My breathing quickened as anxiety flickered in my chest. I felt the eyes of the other students searing into my back. I felt the weight of my sticks in my back pocket. I felt the heaviness of being different in the air all around me.

Gently placing my coffee cup down on his desk, I reached into my back pocket for my phone. Quickly, Dr. Hanover's gaze shifted from his gradebook to my coffee cup, and then he looked at me sternly. His lips were moving too quickly for me to decipher what he was saying, but one thing was clear: I'd done something wrong.

I tapped frantically at my phone, trying to get to my app so I could explain myself. But before I could make any headway, a strong masculine hand reached across my body, encircled the paper cup and lifted it off the desk. My eyes snapped up to Dr. Hanover, who was now looking at the guy next to me, and then I turned to face the dude who seemed to think I needed help.

Of course, it was him, the guy from the silent disco. Because that was how life worked, a constant series of *oh my gods*.

CHAPTER THREE

ZACK

HANOVER WAS IN A SHIT MOOD. Admittedly, he wasn't the most approachable guy. He was intense, unrelenting and driven. I wanted to be his TA for a reason. The guy was fucking sharp. His critical nuance was totally unmatched.

After one semester as his student, I knew he had more to teach me than how to identify which methodological tools were most appropriate for answering which research questions. He was the kind of man I aspired to be, a deeply introspective man who was constantly one step ahead of the rest. That said, someone had clearly fed him sour milk for breakfast because whatever was happening with him had nothing to do with the girl from the silent disco.

She didn't see me when she entered the room. I was sitting where I'd planned to sit all semester, in the top left corner of the class, where Hanover could always see me, even though I remained mostly out of sight to everyone else unless they really wanted to twist their heads and find me. The door creaked as she opened it, and of course I looked up, just as I had for every entering student before her. Instantly I knew her. One shimmering swish of her shiny black hair, and my stomach hollowed, clenched in the same tight ball that had been haunting me since I'd reacted so poorly to her deafness.

I didn't get to explain my shock at the silent disco, and honestly, even if I could have, what would I have said, or signed, rather? My reaction was a totally natural response, the kind of response I constantly controlled. But I let my guard down with her for five minutes and promptly acted like an ass. The training I'd received as my father's son blared like a siren in my brain as soon as it happened. I knew if I was already a politician, that kind of reaction could cost me an election. Slipping into showing my genuine humanity—rather than my usual copiously poised, consciously uncoded, and totally contained kindness— was exactly why I shouldn't dance or drink or act my age. It was why I should have minded my own business and kept myself from assisting her when Hanover started to broil, but it was like I was possessed.

As she glanced at the room with nearly full seats and strode with determination toward Hanover's desk, I felt my skin tighten in reaction to the anxiety that crossed her face. I was glued to her as she turned to face his desk, and I couldn't help but dream of standing behind her, pushing back her hair and touching my lips to the slope of her neck.

My brain skipped when I noticed a pair of drumsticks shoved into the back pocket of her jeans. They kinda lilted to the side, and seeing them there made the corner of my mouth lift. Was she a drummer? A deaf drummer? That was bold, both deliciously and delightfully counter to people's expectations of deafness.

I'd never done anything so counter to people's expectations of me. I'd never pushed back against the edges of my prescribed box, and I found I sort of loved that she did. Respect for her puffed up my chest, like I wanted to stand and clap at her chutzpah. But, also, I was painfully aware that, because Hanover didn't realize Molly was deaf and Molly didn't know Hanover was talking, the situation was about to implode.

Hanover didn't look up. Instead, with his voice tight with annoyance, he practically snarled, "Please take your seat. Whatever question you have can wait till after class."

Of course, she didn't move. She didn't hear Hanover's instruction or the tension in his voice. She shifted her weight and placed her drink on his desk. And just like that, I was up and moving. I was barreling down from my perch, toward the desk, sticking my nose where it didn't belong for the second time in a matter of days because of this woman.

Clearly annoyed, Hanover looked up and snipped at her, "Can I ask why your coffee is on my desk when I've just told you I don't have the time to answer your question right now?"

Arriving by her side, I instinctively reached across her and picked up the coffee, then, after clearing my throat, I used my most professional voice to say, "She's deaf, sir."

Hanover's eyes snapped to mine, the anger in them immediately dissipating. Then he sighed and pushed his hand into his hair, mussing up any semblance of composure. The man was intellectually savvy and had a fierce, argumentative mind, but social grace and fashion sense, not so much.

Grumbling and looking down again, he said, "Right...right... I vaguely remember an email about this. Milton... no." He scanned the gradebook with his finger. "...Mills, Molly. Right?"

He looked at her for an answer. I tried not to roll my eyes as I quietly said, "She can't hear you, sir."

Hanover let out a little laugh. "Dammit. Sorry." He patted his pockets, looking for a pen. It was unbelievably awkward.

I turned to her—the girl I now knew might be called Molly—and slowly signed the letters M-O-L-L-Y.

To my left, Hanover mumbled, "Oh, thank God," clearly thankful for my knowledge of sign language. But, honestly, my signing was rusty. I wasn't one hundred percent sure I'd gotten the letters right. In American Sign Language, "M" and "N" are very similar, and it was possible I didn't know one from the other.

I didn't.

She corrected me. Her nostrils were flared the entire time. It was clear my presence at her side wasn't the slightest bit welcome, but once I was standing there signing, there was nothing I could do about it.

"You don't sign well," she said, moving her hands curtly.

That was true. I should have been angry, but I found myself smirking. Obnoxiously, I took the gamble that I was the only one who knew any ASL in the class. "I'm going to try to help you communicate," I signed, and then, "You're right. I don't."

Her face mimicked my devilish grin as she signed, "I read lips, asshole."

"What did she say?" Hanover asked.

I winked at her quickly and then made sure my lips were still facing her when I said, "This is Molly Mills, sir. She can read lips if you face her and speak clearly."

Molly rolled her eyes at me.

"Wonderful, wonderful," Hanover was still mumbling. "Um… where is your interpreter?"

Molly lifted her hands and shrugged at him, clearly signaling that she had no idea.

Hanover gently closed his eyes, scowled, shook his head and sighed. The compilation of movements and sounds was the equivalent of saying *fucking constant incompetence*. Instead of actually saying that, he heaved a breath and looked at me. "I guess you'll assist her today. And we will figure it out from there."

Molly started shaking her head no, but I gave him a curt nod, and then, making sure she could see my lips, I said, "Of course, sir. I'll be happy to work with her as long as I'm needed."

Her nostrils flared again, she scoffed, and her hands started flying. I only caught a word here or there. They were colorful: *Bad idea. Dumbass. Learn. Important.* Needless to say, I got the drift.

"What is she saying?" Hanover asked.

I pointed to Hanover as I said, "She's upset about the lack of an interpreter."

She shook her head at me, then turned to him and pointed at me, vigorously shaking her head no.

He sighed again. "Unfortunately, Ms. Mills, I don't have another solution today. I'm sure we can get it worked out, but for now, Mr. Worthington is your only option."

Molly blew angrily out her nose like a huffing bull. But then, resigned to the situation at hand, she consented with a little nod.

Hanover looked back to his gradebook and shooed us to our seats. Chagrined, Molly started to move, but I knew she needed more than just me, so I grabbed her shoulder and stopped her. She was watching my face as I said, "Sir, we will have to sit close to you, and you will need to face Molly when you speak."

Hanover's eyes narrowed in confusion. "Aren't you interpreting?"

"Not exactly. I'm not an interpreter. I can't sign quickly. I will need to take notes for her—while she tries to read your lips." I held Molly's eyes as I spoke, watching them soften as I stood up for what she needed. I didn't know what I was doing. I didn't understand why I was driven to be near her and tease her, but I knew I also wanted to make sure she wasn't lost in Hanover's class. I wanted to help her, and I had this oddly visceral need to make sure she didn't hate me.

Hanover got it. He pointed to the two students sitting closest to where he usually paced while lecturing and prodding the class and gruffly said, "Move."

Compliant, the other students started to pick up their things, and I held my arm out in an attempt to chivalrously usher Molly toward their seats. She rolled her eyes at me and shook her head. It was the second time she'd dismissed me.

My inner Han Solo cheekily teased me, *methinks the lady doth protest too much.* And I found myself grinning as I ran up to where I'd been seated to grab my things and then made my way back down to sit next to her.

There was no additional exchange between us before Hanover began class. He was nothing if not prompt and organized. So, Molly's accommodations had him moving quickly to regain his lost ground, all the while assimilating the new parameters of his work. (This meticulousness to detail was what I wanted to learn from him.) He made a valiant effort to face Molly, and, any time he didn't or couldn't, she read what I was typing over my shoulder.

I was constantly aware of how close she'd pulled her chair to mine. Keeping my knee from touching hers was like fighting a magnetic force field or a tractor beam, like my skin was literally being pulled in her direction. And I could smell her, this sort of lightly floral soapy smell. Maybe it was her shampoo or her body wash or whatever; all I knew was that it was intoxicating.

If I took too deep a breath of her, I lost my train of thought and forgot what I was doing. Then, she'd elbow me in the ribs, and I'd feel the rush of embarrassment under my skin as I returned to the work of typing every word out of Hanover's mouth. Literally, it was the slowest hour and ten minutes of my life. But it was also thrilling. Something about being near Molly made me feel lit from the inside. And I wanted to be near her more.

When class ended, Molly stood, pushed in her chair, and, without so much as a wave or a thank you, she was walking away. I jumped up to follow her, leaving my things on the desk. Jogging just a little, I caught up to her quickly and blocked her egress by jumping in front of her.

"I want to send you the notes," I said while signing "email."

She took her phone out of her back pocket, typed into it, and it spoke for her in a tinny robotic voice, "It's confusing when you say one thing and sign another."

I nodded with understanding. "I won't do it again." I pulled my phone from my back pocket and held it out to her, suggesting, "You can put your info in…"

There was a beat, like a long, ugly pause. It felt like a test. She peered at me, and her scolding eyes said, "What's your game, dude?

I tried to keep my composure, my well-practiced calm, relaxed jaw, half smile, but apparently Molly Mills was my fucking kryptonite because, instead, after just a couple of seconds, I goofy-grinned, like forced smile full of teeth, awkward for everyone, goofy-grinned.

Molly hmmphed out half a laugh, and then she took the phone.

CHAPTER FOUR

MOLLY

I TEXTED Coraline an SOS after leaving Dr. Hanover's class, and a day later, I was freezing my booty off waiting for her on the front stoop of my dorm because I wanted her gigantic demanding personality with me at the Student Accommodation Office when I complained about their failure to manage the notetaker/interpreter issue in my Research Methods class. Still, I should have known better than to wait for her outside in the New England permafrost. Cora was my closest friend at school, so no smack intended, but her lateness was a chronic and incurable condition.

She and I met last year during orientation at a freshman meet and greet event that was dumb. No one wanted to be there, but as newbies, everyone felt obligated to do what they told us to do. I had an interpreter with me, provided by the school, of course. As one would imagine, starting your freshman year of college being followed around by an interpreter wasn't the easiest way to make friends, but that was kinda my only choice, so I tried really hard to just go with the flow of being the spectacle.

Only on that particular night, my intended vibe was off because my interpreter was a totally unprofessional jerk. I could tell from the way people were responding to me that he was taking liberties with his interpretations. I was just about to tell him as much when an unusually tall blonde with tight fuzzy curls interceded. I could see she was yelling at him, and I knew exactly what she was saying because she signed the whole time. She started with "OMG. You are exactly the kind of asshole I hate," and she ended with, "Just repeat what she said, dumbass; that's your job."

Coraline's little brother was deaf. Her whole family spoke fluent ASL. Growing up around the Deaf community and loving someone who was deaf made her perception of deafness different from other hearing people. She didn't see me as less than or ask me questions like, "Do you wish you could hear?" She was amazing—the kind of friend who would really be there for you. I was capable of managing my shit on my own, but with an issue like the lack of interpreter/notetaker in Dr. Hanover's class, I was happy to have Cora with me, not because she could interpret for me, but because she was a fucking ball buster. You didn't get pushed around when Cora was on your side.

So far, I'd had little to no response to my emails regarding the lack of accommodation in Dr. Hanover's class, so the plan was for Coraline and me to march on down there and get the whole thing situated because Zack Worthington was not a suitable replacement for a professional. Not that he was totally incompetent. He actually did a pretty good job taking notes. And I was open-minded enough to notice that he advocated for me in a real way. But I could not, under any circumstances, have Zack assist me.

He was an ass. His signing was terrible. He constantly confused words and letters. I was one hundred percent sure he only got half of what I signed to him, and it was possible he understood even less than that. He was pushy and irritating and annoyingly attractive. His goofy grin was frustratingly disarming. As were his text messages, which he had been sending every few hours since I'd given him my number. The first one buzzed through before I'd even left the classroom. I still had my phone in my hand because I'd just used it to talk to him.

Unknown number: I'm Zack Worthington bee tee dubs.

Another text buzzed in almost immediately following the first one:

Unknown number: I can totally see your stick(s).

What was it with guys and cheesy jokes? In less than two hours, I'd rolled my eyes at Zack so many times, I'd totally lost count. Still not wanting to put tons of effort into my response, I looked back over my shoulder to where I'd left him standing and rolled them again. He shot me the same dopey smile that made me give him my number in the first place. That smile of his, the one that sort of exploded onto his face like he had no control over it, I was a sucker for it. Something about it felt like it was just for me. But I knew better.

Zack Worthington was trouble. I could smell it on him. He was the hearing guy my parents warned me about. The kind who saw difference as a trophy he needed to acquire. But if Mr. Worthington thought I was going to be the deaf girl notch on his belt full of conquests, then he had another thing coming.

So, rather than engage, I looked away, recentered myself, and kept walking without texting back. A few minutes later, despite my better judgment, I clicked the info button and added his name to my contacts. I needed to know when it was him bothering me, right? What I didn't expect was that he was going to bother me so regularly.

Initially, he was perfunctory.

Zack: What's your email so I can send you the notes?

Molly: Mmills@qmail.com

Zack: So creative.

Zack: Sent

Then, an hour later, he started to veer off course.

Zack: Are you a music major?

I didn't answer him.

Zack: If you are, you must get shit about it. People don't know how to process things that defy their expectations.

I couldn't help but think that was sort of insightful, but I still didn't answer.

Zack: I avoid defying people's expectations. Easier that way.

That made me stop. Something about that line didn't jibe with the Zack Worthington I'd conceptualized in my head, but still I didn't answer.

After a significant pause, he added:

Zack: Not sure why I told you that. Are you a witch, Molly Mills?

That made me smile, and then I sent back one word, the silencing incantation from *Harry Potter*.

Molly: Silencio

I didn't think he'd get the reference, but he did.

Zack: Good try, Hermione, but I'm not making any sound.

Molly: Touché, Malfoy. Touché.

Zack: Malfoy?? You're a real snot nose, Mills.

And then he was gone. For a while. Later, when I was in the cafeteria eating dinner with Cora, he sent another text.

Zack: How can you eat that crap?

Upon reading it, I glanced around, looking for him. Obviously, he was watching me, which was probably coincidental, but also a little creepy. It was the creep factor that had me typing, I swear.

Molly: Are you following me?

I looked up again to scan the room. From across the table, Cora quirked her head at me. Then she signed, "Who's texting you?"

"No one," I shot back, nonchalantly shrugging as I signed.

Her eyebrows pulled together skeptically. My phone vibrated on the table again.

Zack: Despite you likening me to Draco, I'm not a menacing stalker, Mills. I was just in there getting a soda and saw you, but I figured your tall blonde friend's opinion of me was probably even more god awful than yours.

I let out a sigh, thankful he wasn't around.

Zack: Unlike you, Granger, I am very unwizardly—otherwise I could have just Obliviated her—completely removing her memory of my blundering the other night.

I smiled at that and then wondered why he had such a strangely solid knowledge of the Harry Potter books and incantations.

Again, I didn't respond, but I found myself holding my phone gently, like I was cradling something valuable. Cora was looking at me, narrowing her eyes.

"Is that a boy?" she asked, moving her hands slowly and furrowing her brow in an exaggerated manner. She was making it clear that no matter what I answered, she was gonna assume I was flirting with a man.

I chose not to answer either of them. I just closed my phone and put it on the table. Then, I picked up my fork and shoveled food into my mouth. My best move was ignoring them both.

I didn't look up at Cora, but in my peripheral vision, I could see what she was signing: "Don't play deaf with me, Molly."

I continued to stare at my plate like she wasn't there. But because Cora is Cora, she grabbed her roll off her bread plate and threw it at my head.

I looked up and scrunched my nose at her before signing, "It's no one."

She lifted her eyebrows incredulously and dramatically rolled her eyes, then she brought her index finger to her lips and pulled it away, which was the sign for "true," but it was also how deaf people sarcastically said "sure." Basically, she was calling me out, but I didn't take the bait.

I just smiled at her. She shook her head, and I realized the smile on my face mirrored Zack's dopey grin. Annoying.

After that, all was quiet on the Zack front until the next morning, which was one of the reasons I was up, ready and sitting on the ice-cold stoop.

At the ungodly hour of 7:55 a.m., he texted again: a photo, a sunrise selfie.

He had obviously been out for a morning run, and he'd posed in such a way that it looked like the sun was rising out of his hand.

Zack: Incinedio. Your wizardly ways are contagious, Ms. Mills.

That was all. He didn't seem to have any expectation that I'd respond. I lay in the shade-drawn darkness of my little metal bed in my single dorm room and looked at the picture of him. Because he was backlit, his face was all in and out of the shadows, but the image was clear enough, my heart liked looking. I liked the hard slope of his Roman nose and the equally stern cut of his jaw. I liked the sweetness in his eyes—the way they looked softly into the camera as if thinking of me looking at him when he snapped the photo. And I liked the playfulness of him.

Too much.

Tossing my phone aside, I got up, grabbed my shower shoes and caddy, and headed straight into a proverbial cold shower. In the spray of the water, and while I was getting dressed, I reminded myself that a guy like Zack Worthington would be a messy mess for me. Just to make sure I didn't forget the reality of that, I FaceTimed my parents.

My mom looked the same as always—like a rounder, older version of me, and my father was tall enough that when my mother held the phone, half his forehead and hairline were always cut out of the image. My parents were as deaf as me. In other words, profoundly.

I couldn't tell you for certain that I'd never heard anything. Obviously, I felt rhythms. And I wasn't sure whether I heard or felt very loud sounds. What was certain was that I was prelingually deaf, or deaf before I had the opportunity to learn a spoken language.

My parents were thrilled. In fact, they had been terrified I would be born hearing. They weren't sure how they would have cared for a hearing child. How they would acclimate to what a hearing child would mean in terms of their relationship to the hearing world. If it were possible, my mom and dad would happily function without ever communicating with anyone in the hearing world. Both of them were born deaf. My mother had a genetic condition of the inner ear, which I inherited, and my father had some kind of in-utero exposure that made him deaf, so their identities and their lives were completely defined by growing up in the Deaf culture.

Basically, most hearing people thought of deaf people as broken, whereas deaf people like my parents considered deafness the defining cultural factor in who they are—like how a person might be German or Jewish or American.

Deafness is their culture, and as a culture, it has its own language, mannerisms and social mores. For example, my parents might throw something at me—like Cora did in the lunchroom—to get my attention. It was actually called bean bagging. And while throwing something at a hearing person might be considered rude, it would be totally appropriate for a Deaf person.

Anyway, my parents believed that deaf people excelled and were most accepted in Deaf spaces, and therefore, they wanted me to attend a university with a traditionally deaf program, like Gallaudet or RIT. And while I totally bucked that advice, which they never failed to remind me, I pretty much agreed with them that dating outside the Deaf culture was not worth it. The communication barrier and cultural differences were just too much. Hence, the call to them post-sunrise selfie cuteness. I wanted the familiarity of talking to people who got me so I could remember that no matter how cute the boy – dating a hearing guy came with struggles I wasn't interested in managing.

Rather than actually telling them that a hearing man was showing some unusual interest in me, I complained to them about the lack of an interpreter or notetaker in Dr. Hanover's class. My mother presented as downright scandalized, and my father shrugged and signed, "These things wouldn't happen if you were at a Deaf school."

In a frenzy of staccato motion and wearing her beadiest glare, my mother signed, "You need to get angry." She stomped as if she were the one going there. "March down there and show them who's boss. Be Deaf and proud."

She was silly, sweet and righteous, my mama. My eyes lifted as I smiled at her, signing, "That's the plan."

"Is Coraline going with you?" my father questioned.

I nodded.

He pushed his hand away from his chin, signing, "Good, you know hearing people have more respect for other hearing people."

I sighed, pursed my lips and nodded. I called to be told this exact thing, and still I found it irritating.

As if a light dawned in her mind, my mother's eyes widened, and she questioned, "What happened on the first day? Did you understand anything?"

I was pretty sure my cheeks were turning red. I tried to shrug it off, nonchalantly signing, "A hearing student knew some sign."

"Like Coraline?" my mother asked.

I shook my head no.

My father pointed his index finger and spun it in front of his mouth. "Who?"

"Just a boy," I signed. "His ASL was very bad."

My father rolled his eyes. "Of course."

"Now he'll think he can flirt with you," my mother joked. I didn't tell her he already was. Instead, I looked at my watch and pretended it was time to meet Cora.

Inevitably, if I called, my mom called back. Once I made the excuse, I had to go outside. I had to at least look like I was meeting Cora. So that was how I found myself in the position of a human popsicle when Cora finally arrived. She was wearing hot-pink knit gloves, and her hands looked like they were directing traffic when she asked, "Why would you wait outside? You know I'm never on time!"

I stood, dusted off my butt and let all the frustration I was feeling show on my face as I signed, "Don't ask."

I stood up and walked past her. She chased after me, grabbed my shoulder and turned me toward her. With a ridiculous face that included raised eyebrows and bugging eyes, she signed, "You know I'm gonna. More than once."

And she did. But somehow, I completely refrained from mentioning Zack Worthington to her. I didn't say one word about him at all.

———

When we got to the student accommodation office, the woman behind the desk wasn't at all accommodating. So much so, I wondered who the genius was who chose to employ this woman in the office of accommodations. First of all, she barely looked at me. She spoke only to Coraline, which was both frustrating to me and to Coraline

"Stop talking to me," Cora signed and spoke. "Once again, this is Molly, and she needs your attention."

Cora interpreted as the woman spoke, "I'm sorry. I'm looking here on the computer, and there doesn't seem to be an issue. Molly has been assigned a notetaker."

I signed, "I was, but she… or he… didn't show up."

The woman looked at the computer screen and then looked up at Coraline again, speaking.

Shaking her head, Cora turned to me and signed, "This moron, who cannot seem to understand that if she will just look at you, you would be able to understand her, said that the issue is noted in the file, but you have been assigned a new notetaker, a student in your class, someone named Z-A-C-H."

I started shaking my head. She spelled his name wrong, but I was pretty damn certain that Z-A-C-H was none other than Zack Worthington. My fingers moved quickly, telling Cora to ask if Zach and Zack were one and the same.

She confirmed that they were. Dramatically, I dropped my head into my hands. Then, furious, I signed to Cora, "He is not an interpreter or a trained notetaker. He is the jerk from the silent disco."

Cora started to look shocked, but then her face took a turn, and her eyes narrowed. Her hands moved slowly, her face looking sour as she signed, "He was texting you in the cafeteria."

In my peripheral vision, I saw the lady behind the desk start moving her mouth, and Cora held up a hand, palm flat, signaling for the woman to stop talking. Then she signed and spoke—because Cora never spoke when I was in the room without making sure I knew what she was saying. "Just because you can't hear sound doesn't mean we aren't talking. Would you interrupt a hearing person's conversation like that?"

The apples of the woman's cheeks turned red.

Cora repeated the insinuation at me, only this time, it was a question, "Was he texting you last night in the cafeteria?"

Nostrils flared, I gave her a curt nod of my chin.

Flipping her blonde curls back, she turned to the woman behind the desk and signed, "Thank you. Have a nice day."

And then she spun on her heels and started walking away from me. I assumed she was angry that I hadn't told her about my run-in with Zack. I glanced at the woman and then at Cora's ass strutting out the door. There was no way I could get through to this woman without Coraline—so I chose to chase after her.

She moved quickly. I finally caught up and grabbed her shoulder just like she grabbed mine earlier, but when she spun to face me, I was surprised to find her smirking.

I shook my head a little, not quite able to reconcile her expression with how I thought she was going to feel.

She signed, "You like him."

I did not. I absolutely did not.

CHAPTER FIVE

ZACK

I WAS SITTING in my desk chair talking to Vos and Dickie about some philanthropic car wash a sorority was doing that Dickie thought we should participate in, when Molly texted.

Molly: WTF. You cannot be my official notetaker. Did you tell the accommodations office you were capable of that?

Dickie rambled, "It's win-win, Prez. Money for a good cause, hot girls...

I was only half listening, my eyes locked on the phone screen. I read her words again, and the corners of my lips tipped up. She was so feisty, and even though I knew it was juvenile, I loved getting her riled up. Ignoring Dickie, I typed.

Zack: I did.

Molly: You are a pompous ass.

I started to respond, but Vos interrupted my train of thought. "Zack, do you need a minute?

I didn't look up from the screen but shook my head no before saying, "This is fine. If you want to participate in the car wash, we can participate in the car wash."

"Yes!" Dickie cheered, pushing his fist into the air in celebration.

I went back to typing.

Zack: #fact

I thought the conversation with Vos and Dickie was over, but Vos pushed back, "Listen, Prez, I'm just not sure the car wash is the best choice for our image right now."

"Jesus, Vos. Don't be a fucking party pooper," Dickie whined.

On my screen, the little blinking ellipsis told me Molly was typing, and even though it was contentious, I liked that she was finally in the conversation with me.

Vos addressed Dickie instead of me, "I'm sorry, Dick, but the Beta Phi Omegas have a reputation for mixing social events with philanthropic ones, and right now we are one step away from probation."

Dickie hated being called Dick. Vos and Dickie weren't on the best terms lately, but before I could respond to their drama, the gray bubble appeared, and once again I became engrossed in reading what Molly had to say.

Molly: You are infuriating. This is my ACTUAL life. I have to take and pass this class. It's a requirement. Is it not frustrating enough that my interpreter didn't show and that no one seems to see this as an injustice that needs a solution? Do you also have to make a mockery of me?

Ouch. This wasn't silly play or flirtsy anger. Molly actually thought that with me assisting her, she would fail. I needed to focus on her, carefully craft my response, and I really didn't want Dickie or Vos up in my business.

I stood. "Out." I strode toward the door and opened it for them.

"Yes," Dickie cheered again, annoyingly assuming he'd won.

I snapped, "No car wash. Vos is right."

Dickie cursed under his breath. Vos, who was leaps and bounds more subtle, cradled a notebook to his chest and gave me a little but serious nod on his way out.

I shut the door behind them and crossed to my bed, flopping down before typing.

Zack: I ACTUALLY intend to help you, Molly.

Molly: Please, Zack, tell them you aren't qualified.

I didn't go to the accommodations office to solidify myself as her aide. As I was walking there, I told myself that I was doing my job, that as Hanover's T.A., I was responsible for managing the issue. But that was bull crap, and I knew it. I went there because I felt like it would be easier for me to solve her problem than it would be for her. I knew it was fucked up.

People have agency. They want to take care of their own issues, and solving problems for them is marginally creepy, especially because I hardly knew her. I got that, and still I wanted to make her life easier. So I went there to tell them the situation. I insisted to the staff that the reason I was there was because I was Hanover's TA, and they bought the bullshit I was selling.

The woman behind the desk looked absolutely frazzled. She explained that Molly's interpreter quit last minute, so they didn't have anyone to pair her with immediately. She started to suggest that maybe Molly should just take the class another semester. That was when I blew smoke up her ass and told her I could step in. I wasn't going to lie to Molly about it. But I wasn't totally sure I could pull off the gig either.

Zack: There wasn't anyone to interpret for you. They were going to tell you to drop the class.

I flipped onto my back and toed off my shoes, waiting for her response.

Molly: They can't do that. They are legally bound to provide me with accommodations.

That was true, but it didn't change what the woman explained to me. There was no one to do the job—so even if they found a solution, it wouldn't be immediate, and Molly would suffer either way. I pushed back, trying to help her see that my intentions were honorable.

Zack: I hear what you're saying, but they didn't have anyone, so you were going to have to fight. And tomorrow in class, what were you going to do?

Molly: That expression is dumb. I HEAR what you're saying. You didn't hear what I was saying. You comprehended my point.

She was the best kind of smartass. I wondered where she was standing as she typed to me. Was she right outside the student accommodation office, or had she waited till she got back to her room? Where was her room? Where did Molly Mills lay her head at night? God, I wanted to know things about her. All the things.

Zack: Fine. I grasped your point. Better?

Molly: Not really. You didn't hear or hold it.

Zack: How about gotcha? I gotcha, Mol.

Molly: That's fine, but you sound like a dork.

I snickered. She was funny. I liked her. I wasn't just drawn to her; I actually liked her. I wanted her to like me. I wanted her to know that I was in her corner. I couldn't help but think my father would hate her. He would literally despise everything about her—her punky look, her fiery attitude, her deafness. Molly Mills was not what dear old dad pictured joining us on the campaign trail.

And still, I couldn't seem to not know her. I wanted to know her, to talk to her about the stuff I talked to no one about. Helping with Hanover's class seemed like a good middle ground. My father couldn't fault me for being kind or being friends with her. It wasn't like Molly even liked me. She kinda hated me. She associated me with Draco Malfoy. If I could just help her with this class, then she wouldn't hate me, and certainly after spending some time with her, my fascination would most likely dissipate.

Zack: I promise, it's not a scam or a prank, Molly. I really am going to do everything I can to make sure you pass Hanover's class. I know the material really well, and if I have to teach it all to you myself, I will.

Her little ellipsis started to blink again. Anxiety creeped into my chest. I couldn't remember the last time I wanted something as bad as I wanted to spend time with Molly Mills. I huffed out a breath, sat up, threw my feet down onto the floor and jumped in before she could text me back.

Zack: In fact, I was thinking maybe we should meet up after class to go over the notes together.

The blinking ellipsis disappeared. My stomach flipped. Out loud, to no one, I said, "Come on." Then, I bit my lip and waited.

Finally, the ellipsis reappeared, and I realized I'd been holding my breath.

Molly: Not after class. I can meet on Tuesday and Thursday mornings. 10 AM. In the library.

I was pretty sure Molly thought if she made it inconvenient for me, I'd bug out, but all I could think was I was gonna spend time with her four days a week.

Two days later, I was standing at the bottom of the library steps, shifting my weight from foot to foot and holding two cups—a simple black coffee for me and a salted caramel latte for Molly. In my life I had learned that being observant and proactive could go a long way toward being accepted and liked. Molly brought a salted caramel latte to class twice. It was obviously her drink.

Only, when I caught sight of Molly strolling in my direction, I realized I'd made a mistake. With my hands full, I wouldn't be able to communicate with her. I wouldn't even be able to say, "I got you a coffee." I was usually so poised, so well prepared. But I felt like, when it came to Molly, I was a rookie.

On Wednesday in class, we hadn't talked much. Admittedly, I was tired. The night before I lay awake in my bed, unable to sleep because I couldn't stop my hands from running through my ASL alphabet over and over again. I didn't want to make mistakes. I wanted to truly help her.

Still, Molly remained marginally annoyed with me, but she was pleasant enough, said hello, thanked me for my help before she left and said she'd see me at the library. I was hoping that noticing her coffee choice would win me brownie points. I also had a box of doughnuts in my bag. In college, the bribe of free food always felt like a good one.

Her dark hair caught the light of the winter sun as she got closer, and my heart started to pound. When she spotted me, she didn't smile, but she also didn't frown. I didn't know it was possible, but arguably, Molly Mills had a more practiced game face than I did.

When we made eye contact, she signed, "Coffee, for me?"

I shifted, reaching out in her direction with the coffee intended to be hers. She shook her head no and then, smirking, signed, "I think you should carry it."

My eyes fluttered closed for a second, and I pulled a little breath in through my nose. I wasn't sure if I should insist she take the coffee or allow her to tease me, but she didn't give me a choice. She strutted past me toward the library door. Grabbing the handle, she went on through, just barely giving me enough time to follow behind her without the door smacking me in the ass.

I called ahead and reserved a study room for the two of us, so I wasn't surprised when Molly headed for the information desk, but I watched in awe as she started signing to the young male librarian who seemed to know her better than I did. He wasn't a traditionally handsome dude, but he had a certain nerdy appeal; that cardigan sweater professor thing gets some girls going.

Molly's hands moved quickly, and her mannerisms followed. She was completely different with him than she was with me. When Molly signed to me, she moved her hands slowly, making sure to emphasize each letter or word. Also, the look on her face was a consistently prickly puss, a never-ending question: *did you get that?*

With the geeky library guy, Molly was a flurry of movements and faces. I'd seen deaf people talk to each other before, and I was aware their facial expressions and body language were often dramatically more expressive than hearing folks like me were used to, but somehow I hadn't realized just how much Molly was tempering herself when she talked to me.

Immediately, I didn't like the guy. I didn't like that he seemed friendly but didn't introduce himself to me. I didn't like that his sign language was better than mine. I didn't like his cardigan or his stupid library science degree. But, mostly, I didn't like that she was herself with him and something else with me. I couldn't stop watching her as she talked to him, her toothy smiles, scrunching nose, lifting eyebrows. Her face was absolutely alive with mirth. And then suddenly, she laughed.

An icy-hot fire erupted behind my sternum. My dislike for the library guy took a radical turn, and I hated him. My breathing became labored, and my nostrils flared. There was no getting around it; I spoke with authority, elitist pompous-ass jerkdom when I snarled, "I booked a study room."

I startled the cardigan-wearing, super-signing library-schmoe enough that he was flustered and fumbling at his keyboard when I said, "Zack Worthington, ten a.m."

Knowing I'd caused the change in the librarian's demeanor, Molly spun and shook her head at me. Then, with utter disdain knitting her brow, she signed, "Ass."

Fuck, how was I ever gonna get Molly to like me when I couldn't seem to act even vaguely civilized when she was around?

CHAPTER SIX

MOLLY

I HAD A PLAN. I was going to put Mr. Zack Worthington in his place. A guy like Zack Worthington was used to everything coming to him easily—and my life was the total opposite. When I moved through the world, I constantly had to explain how the situation wasn't suited to me and have it corrected. So, I figured if he wanted to mess with me, then he might as well get shown how exhausting it could feel living in a world that wasn't built to accommodate you. I was going to show him that his life of pressed pants, starched collars, and mighty ego didn't make him universally qualified for all things. He needed to understand that he shouldn't mess with people's lives like he was meddling in mine, and I was going to take it upon myself to be the one to show him as much.

Coraline had rolled her eyes as I raged my plan at her. When she told me I was just making excuses to spend time with him, I'd thought she was being ridiculous. I had a solid plan—genius even. Only, every time I actually interacted with Zack, he didn't seem to react exactly how I expected.

In our second class together, he hadn't made any attempt to be anything but professional. In fact, I was almost disappointed. My spirits lifted when he showed up with two coffees today. I was marginally impressed that he noticed my drink, but I didn't succumb. I left him wanting and practically ignored him while I was talking to Matt the librarian.

Matt was a nice guy. When he'd started signing to me last semester, it was such a relief to talk to someone other than Cora in the way that felt natural to me. And since then, I studied in the library a lot just because he made it feel like a place where I could be myself. But other than friendship, there was nothing between Matt and me—he was in his thirties, and while some women love an older man, I didn't. I'd never even gone as far as having a coffee with him. He was just one place on campus where I felt more like a person than a curiosity.

I was angry when I saw Matt's face shift from friendly and jovial to nervous and uncomfortable. I didn't know what Zack said to him, but it was obviously unkind. But when I turned to him and snapped, I wasn't really any different than I'd been to him in the past. I hadn't shown Zack much kindness. So, I wasn't sure why calling him an ass cut him so deeply, but it clearly did.

The version of Zack that was sitting across from me in the study room was a shell. The normal uppity bravado that emanated from his every move seemed to melt away, and what was left in its place was a self-conscious and incredibly diligent tutor. He went through the notes from the previous day's class in painfully clear detail, writing out examples and constantly checking with me to make sure the information was clear and well understood.

All of our communication was done via an iPad that he brought with him. He typed, passed the device to me, and then I typed. He typed. I typed. He typed. I typed. He typed. I typed. He typed. I typed. And so on until we were nearing the end of the day's material. It was an effective way for me to learn, and it was instantly and irritatingly clear that with Zack on my side, I was going to pass Research Methods. He was devoted, conscientious and wasn't lying. He knew the material well. I might even get an A.

But somehow, he hadn't really made eye contact with me since I called him an ass. And as soon as he withdrew from me, I realized I liked Zack's pithy snide behavior and that I wanted him to spar with me. I wasn't sure anyone had ever really tried to spar with me in that flirty kind of a way, and while it was somewhat infuriating, it was also kind of exciting. And now that he'd withdrawn, I sort of missed it.

Also, as much as he wasn't looking at me, I was looking at him. We were in the little study room alone, sitting at a commercial-feeling wooden table with rounded corners. The table was so nondescript, I'd imagined it could be almost anywhere, in a hotel lobby, in a police interrogation room, in a corporate office.

The light above our heads was fluorescent and gave off a harsh, hard light that would make almost anyone look less comely. But not Zack—up close and focused, he was downright pretty. He had pink fleshy lips and smooth velvety skin. His eyelashes were long, longer than mine for sure. And somehow he was still totally manly, in a way, and wasn't stupidly ostentatious.

He was tall with broad shoulders and biceps that pressed into the fabric of his oxford button-up. He looked like he commanded respect, like he could stop a fight with one threatening look. And yet somehow I thought, if he wrapped his arms around me, I'd feel completely held. Something about being in the room with Zack—even the sheepish weirdo butthurt version—made me feel safe.

But that was stupid. Hormones. I knew he was a jerk. A smart, finagling, handsome, witty, privileged frat boy, right? But then why were his feelings so hurt?

I couldn't take it. I reached across the table and circled my fingers around his right wrist to get his attention. He didn't look at me right away. Instead, he looked at where my hand was touching his.

In my world, physical touch had all the meanings it did in the hearing world —but sometimes it was also just simply a way to get someone's attention. Reaching out for him was instinctual, a natural way to get him to look up and make eye contact. But as he looked at my hand, I felt the moment shift. I felt my skin against his, the hint of his pulse under the pad of my middle finger, and the tickle of his arm hair against my thumb. I saw the contrast, my long, feminine fingers so close to his thick, masculine ones. My heart started to race in my chest, and like a hammer to the brain, I knew Cora was right: I had a thing for Zack Worthington.

I moved to pull back my hand, but Zack was quick. He flipped the dynamic, wrapping his fingers around my wrist. I was surprised by his movement, and my eyes flashed up from our hands to find he was looking right at me. The hand that wasn't holding mine lifted. He made a fist and circled it against his chest: "I'm sorry."

He didn't say the words; he just signed them. The characterization of Zack I had in my mind didn't apologize often. But there was no question, this sorry was heartfelt. His eyes were pleading, physically wide and emotionally open, like if I didn't forgive him, he might actually break. I was so shocked by the genuine emotion on his face that I didn't respond immediately.

He released my wrist, signing, "You are right. I am an ass."

I laughed, and everything about Zack's face changed. The corners of his eyes lifted, and he smiled that big dorky grin of his. He signed, "I like you laughing."

It was a sweet thing to say. I felt the sentiment physically hit me in the chest, like he'd actually shot me with cupid's arrow. The point embedded right above my heart, and at first prick, it was warm and giddy, making me return his toothy smile, but as we stared at each other, just being open and happy, my stomach started to ache.

I looked down at my lap and swallowed down the glow I was feeling, letting the ache take over. Flirting and glowing and smiling with Zack Worthington wasn't going to help me pass Research Methods or become a drummer. And even if he wasn't the monster my parents told me he'd be, he had heartache written all over him.

So, on a deep breath, I looked up and signed, "You are forgiven, friend." I fingerspelled the word "friend" rather than using the sign because I wanted to make sure he didn't miss the word. I wanted to be very, very clear. There could be nothing more than friendship between Zack and me.

When I got to the letter "d," he narrowed his eyes at me, holding me in his gaze. My breathing quickened, my chest pumping up and down like I'd just finished a run. I waited for him to say something, to snidely quip something flirty that rebutted my declaration that we were just going to be friends. He relentlessly held me with his eyes. But he didn't say anything. He just stared at me, eyeing my face like he wanted to eat me for lunch.

I bit my lip. And watched as the hunger in his look shifted and the left side of his mouth sneaked up into a half smirk. He looked away then, closing his computer and starting to pack up his things before he turned back to me. I read his lips as he said, "Sounds good, Molly."

He didn't sign the words. He looked at me again for a beat before he stood and signed, "See you tomorrow in class."

I nodded.

He signed, "I'm already looking forward to it."

And then, hefting one strap of his backpack onto his shoulder, he left. Once he was gone, I just looked at the empty chair he'd been in and the wall behind it, wondering what the hell to make of Zack Worthington.

CHAPTER SEVEN

ZACK

WHOMEVER DECIDED gossip was a feminine trait never lived in a frat house. Sometime in late February, one of my brothers ran into Molly and me at the Bluesy Bean, a musically inclined coffee shop just off campus, where the baristas were known to sing and playfully deliver your coffee order. It was about a month after I first volunteered to help Molly with Research Methods. Earlier in the week, I'd suggested that we meet in places other than the library. Just for a change of pace, I told her. But the truth was I couldn't be locked in that little room with Molly anymore. That little room in the library had become the setting for every dirty thought that passed through my mind.

Prior to meeting Molly, I spent most of my life thinking I was a gentleman. I prided myself on not giving in to the base desires that fascinated all the other men I knew. I thought myself above my animalistic sexual behaviors. In fact, my sexuality was the one part of my existence where I thought I was as morally sound as the sci-fi heroes I idolized. Sex had never been murky for me. Obviously, sex was fun and enjoyable, but only if it was one hundred percent mutual and consensual. For that reason, I liked sex in relationships.

I had girlfriends, not one-night stands. In high school I dated Sarah Wilcox. My father loved her. She was poised, well-educated and came from a lovely family. She had a lot of ballet flats and was very kind. I enjoyed her company. She enjoyed mine. But we weren't in love. We decided to stop dating when we went to college, but we remained friends. It was all very civilized.

My freshman year, I had another girlfriend, Kelly Davenport. She was a brunette. She drank a little too much, but she was good at concealing it. She wasn't as smart or classy as Sarah, but my father still approved. Kelly was from California, and she understood the nature of the press. Her father was a PR man in Hollywood. We dated for a year and a half before she told me that, while she felt I was a good person, she didn't think I cared about her as much as she cared about me. She was right. There was some crying on her part. I didn't mean to break her heart.

In both cases, I felt connected but detached. The only way I could describe it was to reference Data from *Star Trek: The Next Generation*. In my relationships, I was a sentient, self-aware and anatomically functioning male who seemed to lack the emotional component. I could conceptually get that there was an emotion that went with the experiences I was having, but I just didn't feel it. Admittedly, I wasn't totally emotionless; I liked them, but I didn't feel love, or even lust, the way people describe it. I didn't need them or have to be with them. I just liked them, enjoyed their company and enjoyed being physical with them. There was no hunger, no unhinged need.

With Molly, I felt the animal in me for the first time. I wanted to jump across the table and grab her. I wanted to kiss her, push my tongue into her mouth and fucking taste her. I wanted to claim her like a beast, touch her everywhere so my scent was all over her, physically keeping all the other men away from what I wanted to be mine. To be clear, I didn't like it.

Molly made it perfectly clear that she and I were to be friends. And I needed to rein my shit in. So rather than lose my train of thought because, in my head, I'd had her up on top of the wooden table with her legs wrapped around my waist and my tongue down her throat, I suggested a new venue for our meetings. I didn't consider that, unlike the library, The Bluesy Bean would make a public announcement: Zack Worthington spends his time with a deaf girl.

I didn't know the kid who saw us very well. His name was Marcus Wilder. His father was a tech mogul, and he was arguably the type of brother my father would encourage me to befriend. In the moment, Marcus gave me a little wave. I flashed him a smile and then turned back to Molly, who signed, "Who is that?"

"Brother," I signed back.

Molly looked confused and, flipping her palms up, silently questioned, "What?"

I realized she thought Marcus was my actual brother. "F-R-A-T-E-R-N-I-T-Y," I spelled out with my fingers.

Realization dawning, Molly laughed and I smiled—that damn grinny grin that only Molly brought forth, and Marcus saw it. By the time I got back to the house, there was chatter. I didn't zone in on it immediately. I was busy going about my day, but after a few minutes, I started to notice something was amiss. It wasn't that my brothers were gawking or whispering, but there was something in the air, a kind of uncertainty spinning around me. A group of guys, including Marcus, Vos and Dickie, were lounging in front of the big screen in the living room, but they were unusually quiet. I stood in the space for a full minute, my messenger bag still hanging on my shoulder, and no one looked at me.

Finally, I snapped, "What?"

Tactless, as usual, Dickie sing-songed, "Got a deaf chick, Prez?"

On a sigh, Vos added, "I didn't even know you spoke sign language."

I looked away from them and reached into my bag like I was looking for something as I quipped, "I am an international man of mystery." I paused for effect, pulled a tube of ChapStick from the bag and then focused on removing the cap before I said, "I took ASL in high school."

"Bet that's some weird-ass quiet boning," Dickie snorted.

Rage percolated under my skin. Dudes like Dickie were the reason the world sucked, the reason someone like me had to pretend to be into sports, beer and every pair of boobs everywhere rather than admit we liked Harry Potter, Star Trek, Star Wars, anything sci-fi, really, and unbelievably sexy, smart and unique women, like Molly. I wanted to be bitter and spit the truth at him, "Fuck you, Dickface. Fuck you and your fucking ridiculous boat shoes." Or worse, puff my chest out, narrow my brows and snarl, "Talk about her again like that, and I'll feed you your own nuts, asshole."

Only, I didn't. I didn't say either of those things because those things would steer me off course. Snapping at Dickie Dick-face Matthews might let my brothers see the real me through a tiny crack in my carefully crafted façade.

So instead, I smirked and acted like they were stupid. "She's in Hanover's class, you dipshits. I'm the TA, remember?" The lies burned my throat.

Marcus chided, "She smokin' in a punk rock kind of a way." I didn't like his interest, but I could have swallowed my anger if he didn't add, "Bet she's a freak in the sheets."

My eyes bulged at him, and I totally lost control. I fisted my hands, and I would have catapulted myself over the coffee table at his jugular if Vos didn't intercede by standing. He turned so his back was to me and his body was positioned between Marcus and me, then said,

"You two are fucking disgusting. That's a person you're talking about, not some trophy for you to collect."

Dickie snickered, "Anyone ever noticed that Vos is a chick?"

There was a cacophony of laughter. Vos shook his head, grumbling "assholes" as he turned to face me. When he made eye contact, he gave me a little almost imperceptible nod and then strode out of the room. Rather than let me lose my cool, Vos took the bullet. The fire in my chest vanished, replaced by the hollow sting of fear. In my world, kindness never came for free.

Two days later, I was back at The Bluesy Bean sitting across from Molly. Every time I looked at her big doe eyes, I felt like a shit because I made my brothers think she was some teaching assistant assignment. I kept trying to justify my lies in my head because I was assisting her in Research Methods, and Hanover appreciated my effort and lightened my grading load because of my work with her. But I wasn't helping Molly to impress Hanover or as a service assignment. I was helping Molly because I wanted to be close to her. There was nothing sanctimonious or honorable about my behavior. Nothing.

Acting like Molly was just work felt demeaning, like I was an 80s teen movie jock who fell for the nerdy bookworm and was embarrassed to tell his friends. Only in this scenario, I was pretty sure I was the nerd and Molly was the cool kid. Sure, I was pretending to be the popular guy, but sooner or later someone was gonna figure out that I was a fraud.

Because I felt like an ass, I was ridiculously overprepared for our meeting, and Molly was annoyingly distracted. I would go through a point with her, only to realize she wasn't watching me at all. Finally, I put down the iPad and stylus I used to draw examples on the screen and scowled at her until she realized I wasn't working.

When she turned her attention back to me, I was tapping my fingers on the table like some pent-up schoolmarm—which was un-hilariously accurate.

"Shit, sorry," she signed, sighing out a little pressured breath that had me wondering what kinds of sounds Molly made when she was being touched.

"What's up with you today?" I signed and mouthed the words. When we first started working together, I used my voice and tried to sign, but now, in the open air of the café, I felt weird speaking out loud when she didn't respond in kind. I felt like my one-sided conversation would make people turn and look, like I would be calling attention to us.

She shook her head and fidgeted in her seat. "It's nothing," she signed.

I rolled my eyes. "Don't do that stupid shit where you say, 'I'm fine,' but you're totally not fine at all. It's annoying, and I don't have patience for it." I had started to get more performative when we spoke, making more expressive faces and movements like she did. I wasn't quite as flamboyant about it, but I was definitely more demonstrative than I'd been when we met.

Still, I was surprised when she giggled at me.

"What?" I asked, palms up, shifting my hands in front of me.

She mimicked me, signing, "I'm fine," shifting her shoulders and her hips in her seat. The movement was very righteous lady swagger.

"I did not do that," I signed.

She vigorously pumped her chin up and down before saying, "Oh yes you did."

"Whatever," I said, forming a "W" by putting the tips of my two thumbs together and pointing my index fingers at the ceiling. "You are avoiding the original question."

She puffed out a heavy breath and then reluctantly admitted, "I have a show on Friday."

I was instantly excited and endlessly curious, and, as was my way with her, I could barely contain my sentiments. My hands flying, I blurted out, "Really? Where?"

"At the concert hall in the music department. It's not a big deal. It's just a casual performance. It'll be mostly music majors and their friends."

And me, I thought but didn't tell her. Instead, I questioned her, "Why is this casual show making you so distracted? I thought you loved playing the drums."

"I do," she signed emphatically, but by the way her eyes shifted away from me, I could see she wasn't telling me the whole story.

I leaned back in my chair and crossed my arms over my chest, waiting for her to spill.

"It's personal," she signed.

I still said nothing, just popped my eyebrows and pursed my lips, implying I didn't care if it was personal. I still wanted her to tell me why she was upset.

This time she rolled her eyes at me before signing, "Fine. People..." She made a peace sign with her fingers and moved them in a circle while sort of pointing at me. I didn't know the sign. My brow furrowed. I hated that she was telling me something personal, and I was failing to understand.

Grasping my confusion, she spelled out "S-T-A-R-E."

"So?" I questioned. "Isn't that what audiences are supposed to do?"

"They stare because I'm Deaf." She sighed as she signed. "Don't get me wrong. I am proud to be Deaf. It's who I am. I wouldn't have it any other way. I'm not flawed in any way, but I hate that other people perceive me that way. I hate that when I play, I'm the deaf drummer, an O-D-D-I-T-Y or a S-P-E-C-T-A-C-L-E. For hearing people, my drumming is invisible in the context of my deafness. It's irritating."

I shook my head no.

"No?" she questioned, smiling a bit at my response.

As a politician's son, I absolutely didn't agree with her assessment. She had to reframe. This was about how she chose to spin their attention. "You are looking at this in the wrong way."

"Really? And you, a hearing man, have the ability to tell me what my experience feels like?" she smarted, giving me a look that screamed sarcasm. My defiance and inability to accept her perspective was starting to annoy her. But I didn't care.

"I'm sure," I began, "at first the fact that you are deaf and a drummer draws attention. But you get to choose what to do with that attention. You can hate that they see you as an oddity, or you can show them that your deafness is invisible in the context of your drumming."

She quirked her head at me as if she were thinking, and then she signed, "You're wrong, like completely, because my deafness should never be invisible, Zack. It's part of who I am." For a second I felt stupid and awkward, but she didn't leave me wriggling for long. "That said, what you're trying to say isn't totally without merit. When I am playing, they should see that my deafness makes me the drummer that I am. That it allows me to know the music in my way, and that is powerful."

"Yes, that," I signed, smiling at her, feeling gracious that she attributed any of her revelation to me.

She looked at her lap, and she hid her face from me, but I could see she was smiling. When she looked up again, she brought her fingers to her lips and then tipped them at me palm up, like she was tipping a hat. "Thank you for noticing my mood."

"You're welcome," I shrugged, basking in the glow of playing some role in her feeling better, and then I added, "Also, Mol, I'm guessing that most people aren't staring because you're deaf." She shrugged. Again, when this girl was around, I was completely devoid of any social grace whatsoever, so I simply noted, "They're staring because you're beautiful."

Molly's pretty full lips parted, and somehow her giant eyes grew even more giant right before the apples of her cheeks pinked, but unlike all the women I'd known, she didn't try to sluff off the compliment by denying it or by returning with a similar sentiment about me.

Instead, she just gathered her wits, rolled her shoulders back, thanked me a second time and then adorably winked before signing, "Don't we have work to do? I need to pass this class, you know?"

———

On Friday, I bowed out of my fraternity activities. My brothers were doing something raucous as usual, a *Risky Business*-themed party, where everyone wore oxfords, Ray-Bans and underwear. It was clearly something I should have been around to supervise, but I couldn't stop myself. I had to see Molly play the drums. I knew how passionate she was about her music, and I was possessed by the need to see her focused on the thing she loved.

So, I lied. I told Vos I had a paper to finish and asked him if maybe, just this once, he could stand in for me. I'd never asked for his help before. Ever. I'd never really asked for anyone's help, so I was prepared for him to say no way or not a chance.

But he just smiled and said, "Anytime." The simplicity of his kindness stunned me. I must have looked perplexed because he gave my shoulder a squeeze. "We're brothers; that means we've got each other's back."

I gave him a curt nod, started to walk away and then thought better of it. Turning to him, I said, "Thank you, Vos."

He smirked at me and then chuckled to himself. "You should be thanking me. Keeping the assholes in this house in line is a big freaking favor."

He was joking, but since I met Molly, I'd become astutely aware of Vos's loyalty to me—not my father or my clout—just me. He looked out for me, and while I was hesitant to trust him, I was also hopeful that maybe there were others who didn't really fit the mold. People who were different like me, who hated conforming to what was expected of them. Or just people who were kind and caring and motivated by goodness rather than success, power and personal desire. It seemed unlikely but not impossible.

I considered making a show of my lies, packing a backpack so I looked like I was going to the library, but then I decided I didn't care. My brothers could think what they wanted, and honestly, I wasn't sure most of them were observant enough to notice that I left fancy-free and unencumbered. In the cool dusk air, I made my way across campus to the building that housed the music department, theater department and the different university performance spaces.

There was a state-of-the-art performing arts center with seven hundred odd seats, but that wasn't where Molly's band was playing. She was in the Keller Theater, a smaller auditorium with chairs that got stacked up along the walls after each performance so the space could also be used for dance and orchestra practices. I'd been there before. It was a very tan space: tan walls, tan stage, tan chairs. The consistency of color was off-putting, and something about it reminded me of a green-screen stage or the holodeck on *Star Trek*. Whenever I'd seen a performance there, I'd felt like the space was intentionally devoid of character so it could transport you to another world.

Only, the performances I saw there weren't particularly transformational. If I were a critic, I'd refer to them as, "Meh. Nothing special." But it occurred to me, even before I saw her play, that Molly could be more. Just her sheer attachment to her sticks told me that, for her, drum playing was sacred. That kind of passion could not be faked. She had drive. It owned her, demanded her dedication and devotion, kept her prone, praying and striving for her own success.

I didn't feel that way about anything. But she did, and I had to see it, be privy to it. So, I just showed up. I had to watch her thrive. She didn't invite me to the show, and I didn't ask her if she wanted me to come because I couldn't bear to hear her say no. I would not miss it. I couldn't stop myself.

I lingered in the hall until the lights in the auditorium dimmed, and then I snuck inside the room and stayed near the exit, thinking I could just sneak away after I saw what I came to see. On the stage in front of me, shadows moved as the musicians made their way to their marks. And then, with the dramatic strum of an electric guitar, the darkness gave way to the band's moody silhouettes.

Her drum kit was set up in the back, center stage. She was mostly dressed as usual, ripped jeans and a dark punky V-neck T-shirt, but barefoot. As the other musicians tuned and prepped, she took a deep breath. Her eyes were glued to the band's singer as she waited for his cue. Her concentration, her focus was palpable, heavy on her shoulders like a physical weight. Finally, on the singer's cue, she leaned into her music and began—pounding out the heart and soul of the performance.

I couldn't look away.

CHAPTER EIGHT

MOLLY

AS THE LIGHTS came up over the audience, I could still feel the vibration of the music rumbling through my chest. My breath was labored from my efforts, and there was sweat on my brow. I scanned the sea of people, looking for Cora. I knew she was out there somewhere. She never missed my performances, but I hadn't spotted her just yet.

People were still clapping and cupping their mouths with their hands and probably hollering. I could sense that there was sound, maybe a lot of it, but for me, it was just a vast field of human movement. Shifting shoulders and hips, bodies turning to gather their jackets and purses. Without locating Cora, I spun on my little stool and grabbed my Converse. I played barefoot because having the soles of my feet on the floor made it easier to feel the vibrations of the music.

I felt good. I played well. And much to my chagrin, I knew the ease with which I played was partly because of the conversation Zack and I had. I approached this gig differently, focusing on the task at hand. I chose to focus on the power of *my drumming.* I was Deaf, and I was talented. That was what the audience needed to see. I was a drummer, and when I stood up in that sorta rinky-dink multipurpose auditorium, shoving my sticks into the back pocket of my jeans, pride rippled through my chest as my bandmates smiled and gave me their thumbs-up.

The band I'd been playing with wasn't a regular gig. There were four of us: a guitarist, a singer, a bass player and me. We were assigned to each other in my performance of rock 'n' roll class. When we first started practicing for this show, an interpreter had joined us, but once we'd worked out the kinks and my band-mates realized I could play, I'd started rehearsing with them by just relying on signals from our singer, Joey. Our show was more like a group presentation than an actual gig, but I could tell from the smiles on their faces that they were pleased with our performance, and deep down I hoped to play with them again.

So, even though I had to work to communicate with them, I strode toward where they were congregating at the front of the stage to shake hands and just generally commune over our success. They were welcoming. Patting me on the back and shaking hands, and then, Joey —whom I honestly hadn't talked to much—pulled out his phone and texted the group text we created to schedule rehearsals and whatnot. Taking my buzzing phone from my back pocket, I read:

Joey: *I just wanted to say fuck yeah, Mol. You killed it.*

I looked up at him and smiled, scrunching my nose, trying to look growly and badass before lifting my hand and throwing him a *rock on* sign. There might have been something flirtatious in the way he laughed at my response, but I didn't examine the thought for very long because, as Joey shifted his weight to laugh, I noticed Zack standing behind him in the back of the thinning crowd.

Just the sight of him made my cheeks hot. He was unexpected, and the foolish girly girl, the one who grew up on Disney's white knights and princes, the one who usually stayed hidden in the dark recesses of my brain, was totally triggered by his presence. A swoony, achy feeling blossomed in the pit of my stomach. I knew the music department wasn't his scene. He came to see me, to support me.

I had the urge to hop off the stage and scurry across the room until I was standing in his airspace, but I tethered my feet to the ground by imagining they were planted in pails of hardened cement, reminding myself that no matter how kind or interested he seemed, it was my job to be wary, to protect myself from him, to remember that Zack Worthington and I would never work—a relation-ship between a hearing guy and me was doomed from the start. But that didn't stop me from staring at him.

He looked awkward and uncomfortable. His hands were shoved deep into the pockets of his jeans, his shoulders curled inward, and he was looking at the floor. Everything about the stance screamed, *I don't belong here,* which wasn't like him. Normally, he stood tall, with absurdly proper posture. Zack always seemed to command authority, like it was his job to lead in every situation. For him, something about this moment was different. He looked toward the exit a couple of times, but he didn't make a move to leave. Eventually, he glanced up, and his eyes snagged on mine.

My heart started to rev and purr. *Jesus, I was a car, and Zack's gaze was the key to my ignition.* I couldn't stop myself from biting my lip, attempting to shut down the grin that threatened to break loose. From a distance, I could see his anxiety settle as he connected to me. His shoulders rolled back, and the corner of his mouth lifted. Then, he shrugged, making a silly, sweet, sort of surprised face, as if he were saying, "Yeah, looks like I showed up here. Weird, huh?"

My smile became unmanageable, spreading across my face whether I liked it or not. The phone in my hands buzzed, but before I broke eye contact, I silently demanded he wait to speak with me by holding up a finger and offering a nod, the universal sign for *give me a minute*. Glancing at my phone, I read the text that came in. I thought it was going to be from one of the band members I was standing with, but it wasn't; it was Cora.

Cora: *Zack Attack!!*

Me: *What is he doing here?*

Cora: *Girl, that boy is hot like wasabi when he's next to your body.*

Cora loved the band Better than Ezra and was constantly working their lyrics into our conversations.

Me: *I've made it very clear that we are only friends.*

Cora: *Well then, you should stop biting your lip when you look at him. #justsaying*

I didn't text her back. Instead, I looked up, trying to find her so I could roll my eyes in her direction. She escaped my chagrin by cheekily striding toward Zack with her hand outstretched, ready to shake hello. Not good. Not good at all. Cora was not subtle, and for whatever reason, she seemed eager to push me toward Zack rather than protect me from him. I could only imagine the things she was about to say.

Anxious to interrupt her, I turned back to the group before me—who had gone on talking, not texting. I didn't think their exclusion of me was intentional. They were excited about our performance and talking and listening were their default settings. Still, I didn't plan on standing by trying to read lips. If they wanted to play with me again, they would have to reach out in a way that felt conscious of me and my needs.

I touched Joey's arm to get his attention and waved a little goodbye to him and the others. They were gracious enough, but I remained aware that I was on the outside. I was hopeful that would change, but in that instant, I was more concerned with the Zack and Cora situation.

Trying not to look too rushed, I moved down the steps and headed in the direction of my best friend and my overzealous, nosy, and annoyingly attractive interpreter. I felt him watching me the entire time, and eventually, I looked up and made eye contact. His mouth was moving as he exchanged niceties with Cora, but I was right, his eyes were on me. His intensity gave me goosebumps. Suddenly hot and sweaty, I found myself particularly thankful for the existence of deodorant.

Flustered, I glanced away again, but he remained unfazed and kept staring. You didn't need to be that close to have a conversation in sign language, but Zack waited till I was close enough to make the three of us a triangle before he signed, "Exceptionally talented, as expected."

I swallowed. The things he chose to say were always presented as factual, so a compliment from Zack felt different than other people's praise. Somehow, if he noted your talent, you felt validated, like there was no questioning his assessments.

"Agreed," Cora added. "You rocked it."

Bringing my hand to my chin, I signed, "Thank you."

My comment was followed by a pause. I wasn't sure what to do or say. I looked at my sneakers, trying to decipher my next move. Cora bopped her hip against mine, bringing my eyes up to hers and throwing an expression that incorporated a lot of eyebrows and unabashedly screamed *hubba hubba*. She started moving her hands to explain, "Zack just apologized for the night you two met."

I furrowed my brow and then released it, turning to him as I brought my index finger to my lips and then, pushing my hand in his direction, asked, "Really?"

"It wasn't my best moment," he signed and sighed dramatically. The more time we spent together, the more his body language became expressive for my benefit. It was adorable, and sometimes it made me want to hug him, but I still hadn't forgotten the look he gave me the night at the silent disco, the-wtf-you're-deaf?? look.

"Nope," I quipped, popping my fingers and wrist so my signing and expression were laced with sarcasm.

He laughed, shaking his head at my refusal to let him off easy. Then, turning to Coraline, he signed, "Your friend is ruthless. You know that, right?"

Cora wagged her head back and forth as if she were using her body to weigh his sentiment like Lady Justice. "I'd call it honest or scrupulous, if it were up to me."

"Is that so?" he asked, still signing as he spoke, never losing sight of my inclusion. "Perhaps you could help me out then. How do I go about making amends for my idiocy?"

"You'll figure it out. I'm sure." Cora winked.

Zack fired back, "Could I perhaps take you two to dinner tonight as an act of self-flagellation?"

Cora eyed him, suspicious. "Like a fancy sit-down meal or a slice of pizza?"

Bordering on mockery, Zack bowed to her. "The choice is yours, my lady."

Their whole exchange was ludicrous. It left me feeling both giddy and strangely anxious. The uncomfortable heat that originated in my armpits spread as they spoke and signed. My palms grew clammy, and the back of my knees stuck to my jeans, but still I smiled. I didn't totally understand his interest in me, but he was clearly trying to elicit the camaraderie of my best friend.

"She's not a fancy dinner type," Cora signed. "Take her for pizza."

"Her?" he asked. "You're not joining us?"

She shook her head no and then noted, "I'm gonna lie and say I have plans when, really, I'm going to just go back to the dorm, eat a Lean Cuisine and wait up till she gets back so she can tell me all about what it looks like when you really get to groveling."

He laughed, while I smacked her with the back of my hand. Cora just grinned and took a tiny step back, moving in the direction of the exit as she signed, "Have a good time on your date."

My eyes widened, and I moved my hands frantically, signing, "This is not a date."

She shrugged. "Suit yourself, but if it walks like a duck and talks like a duck, I'm going to call it a duck."

I knew I was full-on blushing when I turned to him. "Ignore her," I signed. "We're not on a date."

He lifted his hand to mine, stilling their movements. His touch was somehow soft but strong at the same time. As soon as I felt the warmth of his hand, I wanted him to touch me in other places, but instead, he spoke clearly, so I could read his lips. "Don't worry, Moll. I know this is not a date."

I nodded, and some of the anxiety that had been percolating under my skin since I approached Cora and him eased off, making room in my chest for the basic function of breathing.

But then he added, "I'm just happy to spend time with you," and the regular intake of air quickly got complicated again.

CHAPTER NINE

ZACK

I TOUCHED HER. I touched her hands. Ever since, the feeling of Molly's satin-soft skin consumed me. It was an instinctual moment. I was just trying to squelch her concern and make her comfortable, but fifteen minutes later, as we crossed over the threshold of my favorite Italian joint, Sunrise Pizza, my hand was still pulsing with the desire to touch her again.

On the drive over, she didn't try to sign to me, and I wondered if that was her knowing I absolutely wasn't ready to sign and drive, or if she was just too nervous and uncomfortable to talk. Sure, our conversations had ventured into the territory of friendship, but we'd never spent a minute together that wasn't under the guise of our professional relationship, and despite the impromptu nature of the situation and what I'd told her, this outing felt suspiciously like a date.

A part of me was elated. I literally couldn't think of anything I desired more than spending time with Molly. I wanted to learn about the details of her life. What inspired her to love music and pick up drumsticks? Who were the people she had loved and laughed with? Where did she grow up? What was it like the first time she was kissed, and where was that guy because I sort of wanted to punch him?

But the thing was, I had no right to feel possessive of her lips. None. Even if this felt like a date and looked like a date, it wasn't one. It couldn't be. Not only because Molly clearly didn't want it to be, but also because traipsing Molly into the world my father shaped for me would only cause her grief. So, no matter how silky the back of her hand felt in my palm, or how physically painful my desire to step into the role of her dashing hero became, I could never be the man who slipped his arm around her waist and let the world know she and I belonged side by side.

With her, I could only have all the friendly things. I could watch her giggle or get annoyed. I could see her passionately whip her hands around as she argued. I could encourage her, get to know her and keep her in my life. We could share a treasured friendship. I could build that with her. I just had to be strong enough to hide and contain the hungry animal that wanted her naked and shivering, with my mouth on her skin.

So, the plan was to eat pizza together. A totally harmless thing to do. Friends shared a pizza. In general, there was nothing remotely romantic or lusty about pizza's hot cheesy goodness. Everybody loved pizza.

Also, Sunrise was a casual kind of place. It was the place you brought the peewee soccer team to celebrate their first win. The ambiance offered up nothing to speak of, just lackluster almond and orange molded laminate booths and tile floors. It wasn't fancy in the slightest. You didn't bring a date to Sunrise. And I was a regular, so it had the added benefit of being a place where I was known, which meant the possibility of being seen with Molly. The threat of prying eyes would serve to remind me to stay in my lane, the friend zone.

As we entered, Max, the guy behind the counter, bellowed a hello. He was an odd-looking, very alternative guy, tall and gangly with piercings and tattoos. I liked him. He wasn't a busybody, but he was friendly and made jokes, so I wasn't surprised when he asked, "Who, pray tell, is this punk princess, and shall I commit her order to memory?"

Not wanting Molly to miss anything, I turned to her and interpreted.

"Punk Princess?" she signed back, rolling her eyes.

Unlike most people, Max took her deafness in stride. When I turned back to him, he didn't say anything stupid or look surprised, like I had.

"She didn't love your characterization of her," I said and also signed.

Max winked and then said, "What kind of punk would you be if you liked being called princess?

She smirked and then spelled out, "M-O-L-L-Y" before offering him her hand to shake.

"She said she's Molly," I offered.

"Nice to meet you, Molly. I'm Max." Max shook her hand. I watched their palms meet, and wisps of jealousy flickered around the edges of my thoughts.

Reading his lips, she smiled, then turned to me before responding, "M-A-X?" She spelled out his name to make sure she'd gotten it correct. I nodded. Turning back to him, she signed, "Nice to meet you too, M-A-X."

I spoke her words aloud, sounding completely normal, warm even, but looking at Max with his stretched-out ears that must have once held gauges, his spiky hair, and chipped remnants of black nail polish on his nails, I wondered if he was the kind of man Molly desired to date, a man who thwarted convention, and the thought made my mouth go sour.

Max caught on insanely quick, signing back the letters of his name. "M-A-X?"

Molly grinned and nodded. She was delighted by his attempt to make her feel welcome. She glowed at him like she had at the librarian the day of our first follow-up meeting, and just like that day, I was irritated, but this time, I fostered a modicum of control and swallowed my jealousy, knowing it was both unwarranted and unwanted.

"How do I say 'pizza'?" Max asked. And at the same time, Em and I put our palms up in front of our bodies, crooked our pointer and middle fingers like hooks and drew a Z in the air with our hands.

"What kind of..." Max mimicked the movement we'd shown him in the middle of his sentence to say pizza, "would you like, Molly?"

She turned to me, questioning, "A slice? A pie?"

"I'll eat more than a slice," I responded. "And I'm generally a purist. Cheese or pepperoni, but I'm open to anything. Get what you like."

I immediately saw the mischief in her eyes. "Anchovies?" she asked.

I thought, *Oh, gross. Ew, ew, ew.* But I said, "Anchovies? Um...Sure."

Behind the counter, Max swallowed a little chuckle.

"Really?" she signed.

"If that's what you like." I shrugged, trying not to picture the hairy little fish bits and swallowing back my repulsion.

Shaking her head, Molly laughed; she was obviously teasing me about the anchovies. *Thank goodness.* And she was utterly delighted by her joke. She enjoyed pushing my buttons, which was fine because I enjoyed her enjoyment.

"You sit," she signed. "I'll surprise you." Then, she took out her phone, and, using her electronic translating app, she spoke, "Max, let's pick out a pizza Zack will hate."

Max let his laughter loose and then, looking at her, said, "I like your style, lady."

I still hadn't moved, so Molly turned to me and pointed to the table in the back corner, repeating the sign, "sit."

I moved to do as I was told, but once I was turned so she couldn't read my lips, I said to Max, "Do not let her pay. Bring me the bill when we're finished." As soon as the words left my lips, I felt shitty about hiding them from her. I knew it was rude to talk behind her back, but I wanted to buy the damn pizza, and somehow I knew that Molly was going to try to undermine my desire to treat her. Friends treated friends. We were celebrating her performance; she shouldn't pay. That was just good social etiquette.

Crossing the room until I was as far away from them as possible, I sat and watched as they worked conspiratorially, passing a note and pencil back and forth until she was satisfied with our pizza order. I was unconcerned. Once anchovies were off the table, I was pretty sure I could survive any pizza presented.

Instead of considering the chaos she was trying to concoct, I just watched her. I'd been watching her all night. It was possible I was becoming a creeper. But I couldn't help myself. I found everything about her fascinating: the crook of her elbow, the way she bounced the tip on the pencil on the counter while she was thinking, the pop of her eyes when she felt she'd struck genius, the speed of her scribbling hand as she relayed her choice, and her sheer joy when Max gave her a thumbs-up at her idea. She was a sprite, a spirited menace who'd spiraled into my life, filling it with wonder and consuming my every thought. Her existence toyed with my sanity. I was sure I looked the fool, gawking at her, but for this one night, I couldn't bring myself to care.

After placing our order, she obviously tried to pay, and Max turned her down. It was a short but vivid scene. There was some argument, an attempt to coax him with sweetness, and then a full-on huff before she made her way over to me, flopping into the seat across the table with her arms crossed over her chest. She scowled and pouted as the press of her biceps pushed her breasts together, unintentionally drawing my gaze to the cleavage that appeared in the neckline of her shirt.

Fuck. I could see the edge of her pale pink lace bra. I didn't expect pink. In my fantasies, her undergarments were the same colors as her clothes, black or purple or maroon. That little peek of baby pink felt like a secret, something real and hidden that only I knew, and the knowledge tore through me as if she'd slipped her hand past the button of my jeans and taken my cock in her hand. I instantly was struck stiff, hard and panting, decidedly unfriendly and in full beast mode, wanting to jump across the table to lick a line up from the pointed V of her shirt to her lips.

Not conscious of the dirty inner workings of my body, she glared at me, unrelentingly annoyed. And then she started whipping her hands around, probably lecturing me about paying and speaking behind her back, but I wasn't paying attention because the cotton of her shirt caught on her bra, leaving the tantalizing pink lace exposed. In an attempt to shake myself free from the desire that coursed through my brain and made me grow thick in my jeans, I did the only thing I could think to do. I covered my eyes. When I didn't immediately uncover them, she banged her fist on the table.

I dropped my hands and looked at her as she signed, "Shutting or covering your eyes when someone is signing to you is very rude. If you don't like that I'm angry or annoyed at you, then…"

I interrupted her by karate-chopping my right hand into my left to say, "Stop," and then I told the truth because I couldn't find another way to explain my behavior, and if I was going to re-find my friendliness, I needed the little pink lacy peek-a-boo to end. "I didn't cover my eyes because you were angry. I covered them because your pink bra is showing, and I had to look away."

She stared at me for a second, and before I could really take in what was happening, her shoulders started to shake, and then she was laughing hysterically. I wasn't sure what struck her funny, and I felt downright confused about it. Was it really so hilarious that I was drawn to her boobs? Offensive, maybe? Unwanted, most likely, but can't-catch-your-breath hilarious? That felt weird.

If she knew how I wanted her, would she laugh at that too? I was sure I looked confused and possibly annoyed because she kept putting up her hand, as if to say *give me a minute to catch my breath*, and she would start to calm down, but the uncontrollable laughter would sneak back up and take her again.

Feeling my anger rise, I curtly signed, "What is so funny?"

She covered her mouth with her hand, trying to physically stem her silliness. It wasn't lost on me that she hadn't fixed her shirt, so I pointed at it and said, "Could you?"

That did the trick; her laughter stilled as she untucked her shirt. Trying not to seem butthurt or insulted, I asked, "Is it really that funny that I found your boobs distracting?"

"No." She smirked at me and shook her head as she signed, "However, your ASL is still not so great."

Ensnared again by the roguish sparkle in her eyes, I rolled my teeth over my lip before asking, "What did I say?"

She playfully spelled out the signs I fumbled. "T-A-C-O! I covered because your P-E-N-I-S bra is showing."

After clarifying my mistake, she started to laugh again, only her laughter was smaller this time. It was a soft, sweet kind of communicable laugh, one that said *laugh with me*, but I couldn't. I wanted to laugh because I could see the humor, but I hated that she was laughing at a mistake I made. I hated that I was such a fumbling doof around her. I prided myself on presenting as flawless and prepared, but when it came to Molly, I couldn't even seem to find my poise. I closed my eyes, trying to breathe past my embarrassment, before I shook my head and asked, "Do I make mistakes like that all the time?"

She teased, while showing me the actual signs, "Sometimes, but 'taco' rather than 'stop' and 'penis' rather than 'pink' were funnier than your usual blunders."

Sitting taller, I noted, "I would appreciate it if you would correct me in the future."

She quirked her head at me and studied my face for two beats longer than most people do before tentatively signing, "Because you hate making mistakes?"

I curtly nodded yes and then added, "Also, because I want to communicate with you."

Like she always did when I admitted she had meaning to me, she looked at her lap to hide her smile. Then she deflected by signing, "The pizza smells amazing."

Pretending not to notice she was intentionally changing the subject, I followed the train of thought her comment inspired. Pizza always smelled good, but the smell was just starting to tickle my nose, so I found myself wondering if it was true that when you were minus one sense, your other senses were heightened to compensate. Obviously, the way she felt the vibrations of the music on stage required a heightened sensibility, but was that a byproduct of training and practice, or did her body naturally feel vibrations in ways mine didn't? I wondered if I was treading into territory that would irritate her. I didn't know if talking about her deafness would offend her, but I selfishly needed to get what it was like for her. I wanted to understand how she experienced the world.

"Talk to me about being a drummer," I signed. "How did that happen?"

Instantly, she rolled her eyes at me. "I found sticks. I hit them on things."

"So, it's a cave woman kind of thing," I signed, trying to keep it light. "Should I worry that you're going to clock me in the head and drag me back to your lair – so you can…" I paused the movement of my hands, trying to get my cheesy joke just right, "…beat on me?"

I didn't get the response I expected. If and when I pulled out a cheesy joke, my intention was strategic diffusion. A good pun or dad joke put people at ease. It made them feel like I wasn't smarter or more manipulative. I was just another frat boy, smiling my way through the world. But Molly was keener than the average bear.

Her eyes narrowed, and she pushed forward, sticking her neck out as she confronted me. "Tell me, Zack, what is so interesting about my choice to be a drummer?

Even though she was smiling, I could see a snarl lingering just below the surface. Molly was poised on the edge, ready to pounce. She was waiting for me to clumsily question how it was possible that a deaf girl chose to pick up drumsticks and make music her life. She wanted me to pigeonhole her, proving that I was one of the shmucks who idiotically underestimated her. Only I already knew better. I took a deep breath and dove into the deep and murky end of the proverbial pool by being honest about my curiosity.

"I've been reading about Deaf culture," I signed. "I'm not sure how to talk about your deafness with you, but I feel like I need to. I feel like if I want to get to know you better, I need you to explain to me how best to understand your perspective so that I can finally stop fumbling." I closed my eyes and took a deep breath, praying that my approach was respectful, not moronic.

When I opened my eyes, her gaze was warm but still wary. She crossed her arms over her chest again; only this time she made sure to position them higher on her torso so there was nothing to see.

"Am I an ass?" I asked, feeling my stomach acids kick up and bubble in response to my own nervousness. "Is my curiosity offensive?"

The tension in her jaw softened, and she shook her head no. Then, dropping her arms, she shrugged and signed, "Hearing people don't get how Deaf people feel about our deafness, and so the conversations are often contentious."

If she could have heard my voice, I would have worked hard to keep my tone even, but when it came to signing, I couldn't seem to hide my awkwardness and discomfort. I was always uncertain of how she would perceive me, and it forced me to be more honest than I liked.

"I don't ever want to upset you, Molly. I just want to know why and how you became passionate about music and drumming. I want to understand how you came to play so well and what it means to you.

"Why?" she asked, still steely.

"I guess I'm interested in it all because it's who you are – and I get that your capital D Deafness is a part of you." The things I was saying felt heavy, like I was spitting pebbles – clunky and uncoordinated. "I want to know you, like really know you."

Eyeing me with suspicion, she repeated her question, "But why?"

I went quiet and considered my thoughts. Why did I want to know Molly Mills? Why was I so drawn to her, beyond the obvious pull of pheromones? The truth was she was amazing. Not because she was deaf; that had nothing to do with it. Molly was brave. She was bold and silly. She demanded what she needed and chased what she wanted. She was everything I was not.

"I envy you," I signed, spelling out the word "envy" because I didn't know the sign.

My answer surprised her. Her face dramatically curled in confusion. "What?"

I repeated the statement, "I envy you."

As if it were a footnote, she showed me the sign for "envy," curling her thumb into her palm, leaving the other four fingers upright, facing her palm toward her mouth and then dragging her pointer finger down her cheek through the crease of her smile line. Then, using the sign, she repeated my thought back to me as a question, "You envy me?"

I nodded. I didn't flinch or look away. I wanted her to know what I was saying was the absolute truth. While others might look at her and let their bias dictate what they saw, I already knew better. Molly Mills was stronger than most. Stronger than me, most definitely. Her deafness was an attribute, a gain, not a deficiency.

"Why?" she asked a third time, but her anger had dissipated, and now she just looked flummoxed. Out of the corner of my eye, I could see Max approaching with whatever pizza she deemed hateable. Before he interrupted us, I wanted her to feel at ease, so I didn't think before I answered. I just blurted the truth: "Because you know who you are, and you're proud of that even when the hearing world makes it hard to keep being you.

CHAPTER TEN

MOLLY

ZACK ATE the Hawaiian pizza without so much as a grimace. I wouldn't have pegged him as a pineapple on pizza kind of a guy, but apparently his palate was more diverse than his look and lifestyle led me to believe. While he scarfed down one slice after another, I found myself telling him things I really didn't tell anyone.

"I always loved music, the pounding of the bass," I signed. "My mother tells this story about how I was a colicky baby, and they spent weeks trying to comfort me, doing all the things that young parents do, rocking me, driving me around the block, letting me sleep on her chest, but I could not be calmed. Finally, she read this article that said sometimes lullabies or soothing music could help. She knew they were talking about hearing babies, but she was willing to try anything. Deaf people listen to music by feeling the vibrations of the sound waves. So, she put on a song with a repetitive beat that she enjoyed and put my bassinet next to the speaker. I calmed down immediately."

Putting down his slice, he wiped his greasy fingers on a napkin and then asked, "What song was it?

"That's not important to the story." I shrugged, trying to conceal the embarrassing truth.

He smirked and signed, "Oh, it so is."

I slumped my shoulder and signed, "Fine, 'Shake Your Bon-Bon' by Ricky Martin."

He attempted to hold back his laughter, but it didn't work. He snickered as he noted, "A spectacular choice. Babies everywhere should so obviously begin their cultural introduction to music by shaking their bon-bons."

"Whatever." I rolled my eyes as I flashed the two-handed "W" with my hands.

His face softened, and he picked his pizza back up, holding it in front of his mouth and waiting for me to continue before he took another bite.

I stared at his lips for a second, lost in their yumminess before snapping back to reality. "There's no great defining moment or origin story here. I can't remember a time when I didn't find peace in making rhythms. When I was a kid, my parents encouraged my love of music. They sent me to a camp with a deaf music program—that was where I first played the drums and learned there were deaf drummers like Dame Evelyn Glennie. Have you heard of her?"

He shook his head no.

"She's this Scottish woman who is deaf and an award-winning percussionist who argues that deaf people can hear music in their own way with different parts of their bodies. I learned to play barefoot from her."

He interrupted me, "You do that to better feel the vibrations, I assume?"

I nodded, confirming his assessment, and then offered, "I know it's a unique choice,

and sometimes I wonder why I insist on climbing uphill when I could do something related to music, like train to be a certified deaf interpreter at concerts, but I can't not do it. I'm a drummer. It's all I want."

Contemplatively, he signed, "Wanting to be a professional drummer is a rough road to hoe in general, but why do you think being a drummer is making a hard choice for yourself?"

I looked at him like he was stupid. "As a Deaf person, I am often perceived as a fish out of water – no matter that I'm talented."

He mirrored my expression back at me. "I saw you play tonight. I really don't think people will underestimate you."

I stared at him and wondered if he was being obtuse or naive? My parents taught me to be wary of hearing people because they rarely saw deaf people as fully capable. And for sure, that was my everyday life experience. But when it came to me, Zack was the opposite of jaded. His vision of the world was all gooey sweet marshmallows. He seemed to believe that everyone would embrace me. It was like he completely rejected the biases and assumptions I put up with in my daily life.

I pushed back, trying to get him to remove his rose-colored glasses. "To be clear, my Deafness is never a hindrance. For a Deaf person, understanding Deafness as a flaw would be like understanding your skin color as a flaw. It's not a flaw – it's an attribute that makes you who you are, but that doesn't stop the existence of racism or bias against Deaf people. Do you really think that when I go to an audition with my interpreter in tow that my deafness won't play a role in whether I get hired or not?"

He shrugged. "Sometimes it will. But if you're the most talented and professional, people will see that."

"That's not how the world works. People often assume my deafness makes me less capable."

"What people?" he asked.

"Hearing people."

He shrugged. "I know you're right. I know there are lots of assholes out there – but you can't deny that you're bold, Mol. You're special. And you never know what happens in life. You don't know who you'll meet or what kind of connections you'll make. For example, I've known Kaitlyn Parker my whole life. Meeting her could change your entire course of action or put you on the path you want to be on."

"Kaitlyn Parker, the composer for Redburn?"

"Yes, and also the daughter of Senator Parker. Her mother and my father work together."

"Umm… wow." I would literally die to meet Kaitlyn Parker, not that he was offering. "That's cool."

"She's cool, and I bet she'd love you."

I didn't know what to say to that, so I shrugged and looked away. I didn't really believe he was looking to introduce me to Kaitlyn Parker. That wasn't the kind of thing that just happened to people like me. It was also the kind of thing a person like him could just nonchalantly say. He was just name-dropping to make a point. And the point reminded me again that he and I led very different lives.

For the second time, he tapped on the table to regain my attention. "When can I watch you play again? Like when is your next gig?"

Even though I was talented, gigs weren't a thing that happened to me every day, which was literally the point I was trying to make, but it so happened that my professor had asked me to play for an alumni event later in the semester during the college reunion weekend.

With cheeks that felt warm and flushed, I answered, "I was asked to play at an alumni fundraiser later in the semester."

"Reunion weekend?"

I nodded.

Tension furrowed his brow, and he grimaced. "I hate reunion weekend."

"Why?" I was genuinely curious. Generally, reunion weekend was understood as fun – full of upscale events connecting students and alumni.

He shrugged uncomfortably and then admitted, "It's high stress for me. Lots of assessing eyes judging me, waiting to catch me mismanaging the current class of my fraternity."

"Do you mismanage your fraternity?" I questioned and then leaned in to take a bite of my slice.

He raised an eyebrow and threw me a cocky smirk. "I don't mismanage anything."

I threw my head back and laughed before I teased, "Am I to believe that Zack Worthington is utterly flawless?"

He shrugged. "Ideally." He paused, cornering me with his gaze before he said, "I'm pretty sure you're perfect, so I'd love it if that was how you saw me."

I shook my head in disbelief, controlling myself from rolling my eyes at him. "Perfection isn't really a thing. You know that, right?"

He shrugged and then signed, "The perception of perfection is a thing."

I gave in and let my eyes roll. His hypocrisy was irritating. How could he place so much importance on people's perceptions of him but glaze over the bias I experienced like it could be overcome with a glass of milk and a couple chocolate chip cookies? Annoyed, I glanced away from the intensity of his stare. I took another bite of pizza and chewed slowly. When I looked back, his eyes had softened. He was waiting for me to say something.

"You're a conundrum," I signed. "Sweet one minute and an asshole the next."

"Don't get confused, Mol." The tiny smile toying at the corners of his lips told me he was flirting. "I'm an asshole, through and through."

I already knew that wasn't true. I called him out. "That's a lie. You're human, just like everyone else." He didn't like what I was saying. His nose twitched like he'd smelled something awful. "We're all messy, Zack."

Now it was his turn to roll his eyes. "What's so messy about you?"

I shrugged. "Lots of things."

He raised his eyebrows and tipped his chin up, using his body language to prod me for actual examples. "Such as…"

I wasn't ashamed of being complicated. My parents taught me it was healthy to be a mixture of emotions, but still I twisted my mouth left and right, thinking about how to express my flaws before they poured forth like a fast, chatty flood. "I wear my jeans for at least a week before I wash them. I judge people who don't like chocolate. That's straight-up insane. I'm obnoxious and weepy when I don't perform well. If left unfed, I'm notoriously hangry."

I expected him to keep pushing. Our default mode was spar, but instead, his breathing quickened, and he looked at me like I was edible. My face felt hot. My hands moved unconsciously, revealing truth bombs. "I'm endlessly defiant and uncompromising – the kind of woman who absolutely has to make her own mistakes…."

"I love that about you," he signed, sultry. *When did his signing get so sexy?* It was something about the way he leaned in toward me and his unflinching gaze. *Damn.*

Trying to shake off his sex appeal, I chuckled and signed, "My parents don't."

He made a face like I was crazy. "I'm sure they are insanely proud of you."

I shrugged. "Sure, but they'd be a lot happier with me if I'd gone to a historically deaf university."

He looked confused. "Why?"

"They feel like I'm missing out – but I wasn't willing to miss out on studying music."

"Do they resent your interest in music?" he asked kindly.

"No," I shook my head, "they just feel Deaf people are safer surrounded by the Deaf community." I shrugged. "But you know, I'm a rebel."

He was too still, staring at me in that way that made my cheeks hot. I watched his chest rise and fall as he drew in a deep breath, and then he offered a satiated kind of lazy smile before signing, "So, let me get this straight, not only are you like a badass who thwarts convention to follow your passion despite all odds, but also you're a rebel who acts against your parents' wishes, does as she pleases, and still somehow maintains a relationship with them?"

I assumed his statement was rhetorical. So, I didn't say anything, but I felt things. I felt seen. I felt like he understood the weight of my choices and how heavy carrying them was when my failure was a definite possibility.

"I'm pretty sure you're a unicorn, Molly Mills."

After all the heavies I just unloaded on him, I was surprised he was able to make a smile break out across my face, but he did. He made me grin from ear to ear, and he set off a carnival of butterflies in my belly.

Zack Worthington was a lot to take in. He wasn't anything like I thought he'd be, and I was definitely having a harder and harder time denying that there was something brewing between us. The way he was fastidious, the way he focused on me and concerned himself with my hopes and dreams. He was bossy and obnoxious, but he was also kind and considerate, and if he was really just looking to add a Deaf girl to his list of conquests, he was certainly going through a lot of effort to woo me. Like, his pursuit would have to be based on a rom-com-style bet-you-can't-get-with-that-one situation for him to take it this far and not have any true interest, and even in that situation, the dude was genuinely interested in his mark.

Still, no matter how sweet or sexy I found him, I couldn't see how we could make it work. Culturally, it was a recipe for disaster.

Maybe a fling? Was that a thing I was capable of? I had no qualms with the woman who sexed it up with no attachments. From my perspective, *Bravo, ladies! Way to get your jollies whenever and however you want 'em!* But sex was a big deal for me. I found opening up to someone sexually made me intensely vulnerable.

Before I was even in high school, my mother started talking to me about how men think they can take advantage of women and girls who have disabilities, telling me I needed to be extra wary. And I knew that was true. She didn't make arbitrary or anecdotal arguments. She showed me studies. It was her way of preparing me for the complexities a deaf woman faced in a hearing world, but the fear she instilled definitely played a role in how I perceived my sexuality. And what I knew about myself was that safety and trust were two things I didn't think I could be sexual without.

I'd only ever slept with one person: my long-term high school boyfriend, Jake. He was deaf. He was a gamer. I knew his family and his friends. We grew up together. I trusted him explicitly.

I didn't think Jake was the love of my life, and I knew we were going to break up when we went to college, but everything about my first time was safe. Our sex was probably best described as exploratory. We learned from each other, but it wasn't the cataclysmic, mind-blowing stuff people talk, write and make movies about. Honestly, I wasn't sure that kind of sex existed. Sex felt good. It was fun and enjoyable, but so were doughnuts. And doughnuts were a lot less messy—emotionally and physically.

That said, the odd mixture of heart palpitations, anxiety, glee and unexplained salivating that Zack elicited from my body was nothing I ever felt before. I wondered what it would be like to taste his lips and feel his hands on my skin. But when I thought about genuinely engaging with him in that way, my brain literally set off like a siren, bleating *unsafe, unsafe, unsafe*. I knew I needed to listen to my brain. It was a good, strong, smart organ. It functioned based on general concern for my well-being. It assessed situations and weighed options before coming to logical rational decisions. My brain's main goal was protecting my heart, keeping that soft fuzzy blood-pumping ball of mush safe and sound.

But there was another organ, one located significantly further south, that annoyingly rolled her eyes at my brain's warning bells and whispered back, *sexy smart hottie, sexy smart hottie, sexy smart hottie.* (I'm talking about my vagina.) Not that I want to make her out to be the bad guy or anything, but my vagina was an intensely manipulative and bossy bitch. She quietly played the long game, never letting up, never reasoning, just continually repeating her point as if there was nothing else to say.

My vagina's consistency was how I found myself in the pizza parlor in the first place, and it was her mumblings that had my ushy-gushy heart feeling open and friendly when I picked up the slice of pizza that was cooling in front of me, took a bite, replaced it on the paper plate and then signed, "Okay, my turn. Tell me something personal about Zack Worthington."

Instead of answering, he took an insanely large bite of his pizza and shrugged at me. I just waited. Cora had once told me that deaf people's innate ability to tolerate silence was excruciating for hearing people. She told this story about how her brother constantly got her to admit her devious doings to their parents by just sitting in silence as they confronted her about things. She explained that his silence made her say things she wouldn't usually admit. Of course, that seemed ridiculous to me, but watching Zack squirm and eat pizza while I said nothing, I couldn't help but remember Cora's point.

Finally, he signed, "My father's a senator."

I tilted my chin to the left, pressed my lips together and shook my head, attempting to scold him with my gaze. Everyone knew Zack's father was a senator.

"Thank you for that general knowledge passed off as an insight into your personality. I feel so much closer to you now." I signed the words with a teasing smile on my face, but after the details I had shared about my life, I actually couldn't help but feel a little put out by his caginess.

He shrugged again and then signed, "Not much to know. Rich kid. Frat Boy. Exactly what everyone expects. A life preordained by the man I call father."

Zack's usually cocky and commanding personality faltered, and he seemed resigned. The shift in his disposition caused his words to fall heavily, smacking their way into my thoughts like the anvils that crush Wile E. Coyote. I had assumed a lot of things about Zack. Nasty things. I was constantly startled when he was kind or considerate, shocked by his ability to provide emotional insight. In my defense, he was notoriously jerky, constantly assuming he knew best. But he was never cruel or ill-intentioned, and I'd assumed the worst at every turn.

Watching him present the finer points of his life in a matter of a few sentences, I realized that perhaps Zack's life wasn't all toga parties and bromance. He had told me multiple times he wasn't like me. He'd said he didn't have a thing that made him feel passionate. But that idea seemed like nothing. I thought what he was saying was—like a million other people our age—he hadn't found the path that inspired him, and he was jealous that I had. But it occurred to me he was saying he felt trapped, that he didn't feel he was allowed to be his own person. He called me brave. He said I was a unicorn. Maybe the choices I made resonated for Zack because he didn't feel he could make them.

My mind raced, piecing together a new and improved picture of him, searching for the pieces that didn't jibe with the perfect picture of American aristocracy. His attachment to me was one issue, but the other thing my mind kept bumping into was his pop culture references. Zack loved all things geeky. At least, I thought he did.

"I have a question," I signed. "What is your favorite movie?"

He answered very plainly with a smile that didn't reach his eyes. "*The Shawshank Redemption.*"

That was a safe answer. Everyone loved that movie. It was a great movie, but somehow I didn't think it was Zack's favorite movie.

"Really?" I narrowed my eyes as I searched his face for the truth.

"It's a great movie," he argued, his eyebrows pinching at my skepticism.

"True," I nodded, "but it's not your favorite, is it?"

He didn't respond. He glared at me, and I glared back. His eyes searched my face, looking for something. I wasn't sure what he wanted to know. I wasn't sure why a person would lie about their favorite movie? Why would anyone feel the need to hide a simple preference? It was bizarre, but the longer he went without saying anything, I became more and more certain, even if he thought *The Shaw-shank Redemption* was shiznit, it wasn't the film he was delighted to see anytime it crossed his path.

"I don't have a favorite," he signed the words quickly and glanced around the room to make sure no one was watching him, like he had just told me a seriously controversial secret. Only he hadn't, had he?

"Why do you look like a spy who revealed something confidential and became a traitor to his tribe?"

He pushed his plate away, ending his love affair with dinner. "If I'm doing it right, then I am supposed to have easy, digestible answers for people's questions."

"If you're doing what right?"

"Being likable. Approachable. Personable." As he scratched his head and took a deep breath, I caught a glimpse of something hollow in his eyes. Something sad and longing, but as quickly as it arrived, it was wiped clean, replaced or covered up by something obviously fake but also exponentially more presentable and uncomplicated.

The transition was downright magical—if you were into that sort of thing, which I wasn't. But it was hard not to be in awe of his complete shift from completely lost to unequivocally confident in mere seconds. As he spoke, he lifted his shoulders and turned his head slightly, so I was almost looking at his profile—but not really. It was like he wanted me to see the strength of his jawline.

"My job is to walk the tightrope of being the leader—strategize better, present utter eloquence and unyielding righteousness, but also bring the jokes and a sense of universal friendliness. Be liked by everyone and touchable by no one."

My only response was, "Ew."

His façade cracked, and the corners of his mouth spread out, revealing his perfect white teeth as his grin spread across his face. Resting his elbow on the table, he leaned his cheek on his fist and gently shook his head at me. He didn't sign the words, but I read his lips when he said, "I can't help but like you."

I liked him too. Despite how irritating he could be, I liked him too much. I glanced down at my lap. I wanted to tell him. I wanted to stand up, walk around the table, slide my booty into the booth next to him and thread my fingers through his, but I didn't. I couldn't. Instead, when I looked up, I pretended I didn't know what he said.

"What?" I asked.

"Nothing," he signed, still smiling as he slapped his hands together to shake off the last of the pizza crumbs. "Should we head out?"

I nodded, still wishing I'd been brave enough to tell him I liked him too.

Back on campus, I expected him to just pull up near the path to my dorm, but instead, he found a parking spot. Rotating the key in the ignition and putting an end to the engine's vibrations, he turned to me.

"You don't have to walk me," I signed. "I can just hop out."

He shook his head no. "It's late. I want to make sure you get to the building safely."

"Thanks," I signed, the movement of my hand somehow bringing my whole body closer to his.

We should have moved, grabbed the door handles and headed out, but we didn't. He just sat there, facing me, his keys balled in his right hand. Because the car wasn't running anymore, the heat was off, and the winter weather quickly snuck in all around us. His eyes dropped to my lips, and suddenly I struggled to catch my breath.

I could feel his gaze like a gentle pressure, making my lower lip tremble and pulse. My tongue seemed to swell in my mouth, pressing into my teeth, desperate to know the feeling of his kiss. I wanted him. I wanted to smell the scent of him as he reached across the center console and devoured my mouth.

I swallowed, trying to calm and push down my desire, but it just flared as the movement of my throat made his pupils grow wide and darken in the bluish glow of the unlit car. This was the moment when my brain lost the battle, and I gave in to the reality that I couldn't control the way I wanted him. Maybe it would be a mess. Maybe it wouldn't, but there was no stopping it. I was into Zack Worthington, and not like kinda.

Still staring at my mouth, he exhaled, and the plume of his breath billowed before him. As if in a trance, he reached up, cupped my jaw in his hand, and slowly, so slowly, he ran the pad of his thumb over my top lip. At the flutter of his touch, my eyes closed, and I sharply gasped, pulling in a gulp of air, my lips parting. The feeling of his fingers on my sensitive flesh made my mouth grow hot and wet, and my heart knocked against my breastbone like it was trying to escape.

The chill around me melted away as I drowned in the heat of his hand. I was consumed by it, the warmth blossoming, flooding my body in a rush of aching need. As his thumb circled around to my bottom lip, I shuddered an exhale, and he withdrew.

My eyes snapped open. My breaths pounded around me as though I'd run a marathon. The absence of him made me feel raw inside, and my chin threatened to wobble. I wanted to be angry, to clamor about mixed messages, but he looked sorrowful when he signed, "My favorite movies are *ET*, *Stormtroopers* and anything that takes place in the world of *Star Trek*. The *Star Wars* films are good too."

I didn't understand him. I didn't know why he hadn't just told me this when I asked the first time, but he was telling the truth, and somehow, it was coming out like an apology for touching me or maybe almost kissing me? Was he apologizing for that? Because, clearly, I had responded in kind.

"Let's get you home," he signed, turning away from me and opening his car door.

Baffled, I followed suit. We walked through the campus without talking, and when we got to the door, he hugged me awkwardly, keeping his distance and patting my back like I was one of his bros.

Not sure what to feel, I took a step toward the door before signing, "Good night."

With my back to him, I scanned my key card and pulled open the heavy door, not intending on looking back, but he grabbed my shoulder, turning me to face him. His eyes were wide, and his cheeks seemed sunken.

If it didn't seem totally out of line with his actions, I would have thought he was devastated when he signed, "For what it's worth, I'm glad you didn't listen to your parents. Knowing you matters to me."

Then he leaned in and hugged me again, for real this time, cradled to his chest, his nose in my hair. At first, my shoulders went stiff. I wasn't expecting the intensity of his touch, the way he clung to me, pulled me close and crushed my body against his.

The chaos of his sudden vulnerability felt like a physical entity pulsing and writhing between us and I was overcome by my need to connect with him, to show him that I cared too. I sunk deep into our embrace, wrapping my arms around him and pressing my ear to his chest, seeking the thrum of his heartbeat, and letting the musky scent of him cocoon around me. For a moment everything was still and calm.

And then he was gone, striding away fast, leaving me to watch his departure.

CHAPTER ELEVEN

ZACK

I DIDN'T TEXT her on Saturday, but I thought about it. I thought about it when I woke up, as I lay in bed and tried to motivate myself for the day. I thought about it when I was pouring my coffee in the kitchen downstairs. I thought about it flopped on the couch in the living room, watching a few of my brothers play some idiotic time-sucking first-person shooter game. I thought about it locked in my bedroom, trying to study all afternoon.

I was still thinking about it when I got in the shower to clean up before joining my brothers for an obligatory Saturday night of beers, burgers and babes. In the shower, I let the warm water rhythmically beat against the crown of my head as I drafted and redrafted what I would say if I had the balls to text her.

Hey, wondering if you want to grab a bite tomorrow?

Nope. That was clearly too much like asking her out on a date, which was exactly what I wanted, but not what I was trying to do. Rewrite:

Last night was fun. We should do it again sometime.

· · ·

Better. Casual, friendly, but so empty. She'd see through that in two seconds. Molly was fiercely empathic. She constantly noticed details about me that others tended to overlook. I couldn't get away with telling her half-truths, but maybe that was my fault. I didn't want to lie to her.

When I was looking into her eyes, I didn't want to be the prick my father intended. I wanted to be the man I dreamed of being—the guy whose moral compass wasn't gray—a hero. Only I wasn't a hero, and I was pretty sure heroes didn't exist.

Truth was, any text I sent would be misleading. She probably thought I was a lunatic. Talk about mixed messages; my behavior toward her was chaotic to say the least. Showing up at her show, telling her I liked her, touching her mouth, and then running off like a scared little rabbit.

If I wanted to recenter our connection as friendly, it made the most sense to either say nothing for a few days, send a text about our work in Hanover's class, or a blasé *how you doing, bud-dy?* text. But, man, the text I was aching to send was so much more than, "Let's do it again sometime." I wanted to drown her in my real thoughts. I wanted her to know that the tiniest thought of her made me raw with need, desperate to see her back bow as I made her come. I wanted to say:

You gasped when I touched your lips, and that sound made me ravenous. I have to know what you taste like, feel the heat of your breath mingling with mine. I can't fucking think of anything but my hands on your skin.

In the end, I sent her nothing. Instead, I went out with my brothers and nursed a bourbon in the corner of a sports bar with my phone on the counter, screen up, hoping beyond all hope that she would put me out of my misery and text me.

In general, when I went out with my brothers, I wasn't the life of the party, so I figured my less-than-jovial attitude would go unnoticed, but I should never underestimate the keen eye of Ashton Vos. I was pretending to give a shit about a hockey game on the television screen above my head when he pulled out the chair next to me and perched there, one foot resting on the bar stool's leg rest.

"Have I ever told you you remind me of someone's father?" he asked.

Pretending to be engrossed, I kept my eyes on the screen, watching the tiny men in big pads and red, blue and white jerseys and skates race across the ice. In reality, I found professional sports uninteresting. I understood why it was a cultural phenomenon. Sports unknowingly fulfilled the average fan's need for tribalism. Football, soccer, basketball, you name it, they were all metaphoric expressions of warfare and aggressive masculinity. In a seemingly peaceful modern world, where there was no need to fend off saber-toothed tigers, sports helped men feel like they remembered how to roar. But I found the whole charade oversimplified and highly commodified. However, I watched because not watching would make me stand out. And, as always, I thought it best to blend in, which was why I showed no signs of interest in Vos's question and acted like the hockey game had me captivated.

Unfazed by my lack of response, Vos continued as though I'd expressed curiosity in his father figure comment. "You never really join in. It reminds me of the few times I've been at a bachelor party where the future father-in-law is present. Nobody knows how to relate to that guy. Like, do you let loose and just hope he doesn't judge you for the rest of your life, or do you give up your last night of freedom as a blatant play for his respect and seeing you as a man worthy of his daughter?"

Sighing, I took my eyes off the screen and turned my head in his direction. "What are you on about?"

He took a swig of his beer and then, with a shit-eating grin, declared, "I'm telling you you're a buzzkill, man." I snickered, turning my eyes back to the screen. "Not gonna lie, you're always the kind of guy who chooses to be the DD, but tonight you're particularly ornery. What's up?"

I shrugged, intentionally being vague. "School stress. Family stress." On the screen, one of the players took a shot and missed, so I responded like it mattered. "Dude. What the fuck? Are they just planning on playing with the puck all night?"

Next to me, Ashton laughed. "Christ, Zack. Don't act like you give a shit about that game for my benefit."

I stilled. Something inside my chest felt like it was slipping, like someone had slammed into my armor, and it was suddenly concave. Apparently, my well-conceived façade wasn't as convincing as I thought it to be. First Molly, and now Vos seemed to see right through me. My voice was stern and low when I asked, "What?"

We were surrounded by our brothers and other people like them. Frat boys and the girls who loved them, throwing back beers, watching televised games and playing pool. The place was loud and smelled vaguely sour. It wasn't the time or place for a deep drawn-out exposé or anything of that nature, but still I felt like I was about to be a victim, like Ashton had been working up to manipulating me all year, and now, when I'd finally started to think maybe he was trustworthy and actually cared for me, he was ready to strike.

He kept his eyes on the crowd behind me as he spoke, "You don't give a shit about that game, Prez. I see you pretending to be engaged in what the other guys are interested in—acting the part of the busted-up fan when a friend's team loses, only to shout profanities when that same team wins a couple weeks later."

I stayed quiet, waiting for the other shoe to drop. I didn't know what he wanted, but there had to be something. There was always something.

"I hate watching sports," he said, surprising me, and then he shook his head. "Actually, that's not totally true. I love *American Ninja Warrior*. You ever watch that shit? Those ninjas are incredible. They're prime specimens of human athleticism." He slipped into having a debate with himself. "Obviously, so are football players, I guess. But the things those guys—and girls—do on ANW. It's nuts—like borderline unnatural. Also, something about the campy contrivance of the competition keeps me grounded in the entertainment aspect of the whole deal… so…I don't know, I just don't—"

I finished his sentence for him, "...slip into forgetting that it's not really important in the grand scheme of things."

He pointed at me. "Exactly." He was smiling, and I was confused. He shook his head at me. "Lighten up, dude. No one really gives a fuck if you like sports or physics or anything else…" He paused, and, dropping his voice to make sure our conversation was totally private, he added, "Like, for example, a certain punky little pixie of a woman."

People cared. He was wrong. My father would care. Dickie Matthews and all the people like him would care. But, shockingly, Vos didn't seem to care at all. There was always the possibility I was blatantly wrong, but he hadn't threatened to expose me. It seemed he was really trying to be my friend, that he was a decent guy who didn't have ulterior motives. His genuineness left me doubly baffled. Firstly, I had no idea how to relate to him, and secondly, I was stupefied to find that I only knew how to pretend to be someone's friend. If we weren't playing roles, then what were we supposed to talk about?

Did I admit to him how I felt about Molly? Could I trust him with that information? If I did, would it be too much to query him about what kind of text I should send her? Or would whining about my feelings for some girl I didn't think I could have make me look like a pussy and make him reconsider being my confidant, therefore exposing me once again to the threat that he'd share my personal turmoil?

Honestly, why did he even want to befriend me? Had I ever shown him the kindness he regularly showed me? And if I had—when did that happen? The only thing I could think of was that I valued his intellect. I knew him to be smarter than my other brothers, and I had always treated him as such, but was that a friendship?

I played coy. Pretended I didn't know what he was talking about while clearly knowing what he was talking about. Lifting one corner of my mouth to smirk and thinking about what it felt like when her big puppy dog eyes searched my face for meaning, I asked, "What pixie? I don't know any pixies."

He laughed without opening his mouth and took a swig of his beer. "Yep. There is totally no reason I see you practicing your ASL alphabet in your lap —*all the fucking time.*" He emphasized his last four words and then added, "I'm not even sure it's voluntary at this point."

Shaking the rocks in my glass, I offered him a plausible explanation, "Constant finger movement is great for grip strength. Maybe I'm thinking about becoming one of those ninjas you're so enthralled by?"

"Of course," he nodded, "and that paper you had to work on last night that didn't require a book or a backpack or a laptop, not even a pen. You just wrote in your head, I'm guessing."

Caught in my lie, I ran my hand over my face and blew out a stream of hot air. "Fuck, man. I'm sorry. I shouldn't have lied."

Vos turned his stool so he was facing the bar and hailed the bartender to signal that he wanted another beer. While he waited for her to bring it, he rolled his neck and said, "No, probably not. Lying is dumb. But I get not wanting the guys to know about your personal life. Especially when you aren't sure about it yourself, which you're not, right?"

"What personal life?" I smarted.

"Fuck, I thought I had you that time." He smirked.

I didn't know what made me do it, but everything around us seemed to go still as I suddenly blurted the truth at him, "I don't want to fucking hurt her."

He was quiet for a beat before he said, "But you can't stay away."

I nodded.

"Well, what if you didn't hurt her? What if you made her happy instead?"

CHAPTER TWELVE

MOLLY

Hey, I don't know what you're doing this afternoon, but I was thinking maybe we could go downtown. There is a store I want to take you to.

Unsatisfied, I passed the phone across the table to Cora without sending the text message and signed, "What about this?"

She rolled her eyes at me and pretended to gag. We were in the cafeteria, and after thirty-six hours of hounding, she finally convinced me to contact Zack. His behavior on Friday night was odd, to say the least, but Cora felt I was missing a piece of information. She insisted there was no doubt he was into me. She said she could see it in the way his eyes followed my every move.

So, obviously, there was something I didn't know about that was holding him back from his true feelings for me. I maturely argued he could figure out his issues on his own if he wanted to date me. But Cora kept pushing, pushing, pushing, noting that if I waited for him to come to terms with whatever he was trying to manage, I might wait forever.

"You need to ask him," she signed on repeat like a skipping record.

Part of me knew deeply that I couldn't make someone face something they weren't ready for, but I also really wanted to know why Zack ran so hot and cold? And if I was being totally honest, I wanted to ask him how in god's name he didn't kiss me in his car? *My god, that was intense.* Either way, Cora deserved to gloat because, without her incessant nagging, I never would've considered reaching out to him. And now I was sitting around crafting a text to send. Well, actually, she was crafting the text, but whatever.

Thrusting her tray aside, Cora rested her elbow on the table and went to work. A few minutes passed with me sitting back in my chair, watching her focus on my phone screen. When Cora concentrated, she stuck the tip of her tongue out of the corner of her mouth. I noticed it the week I met her, and months later, I still found the tic endlessly endearing, but I also thought it was sort of hilarious that she took a text to a guy who liked me seriously enough that it brought out her concentration tongue. We all have our priorities.

After a few minutes, she shimmied her shoulders and passed the phone back to me.

Anchovy-hater, I have an afternoon plan for us. Meet me on the quad.

I couldn't help but grin. She was fearless, and it showed. The text was simple and direct. It left him no choice. I took a deep breath, made one adjustment and hit send.

Malfoy, I have an afternoon plan for us. Meet me on the quad.

Once the note was shot off into the ether, I put the phone down and tried to seem nonchalant about the whole thing, even though I was so nervous I couldn't stop my leg from bouncing. Thankfully, I didn't have to feel that way for very long because Zack texted back almost instantly.

Zack: Still the villain, huh? Can't I at least be someone less sniveling, like Kylo Ren?

•   •   •

He was cheeky. So easily. It was like the funny quippy lines just naturally rolled out of him. I really had to work at them. Also, um… what? Kylo Ren was the worst.

Molly: *Kylo Ren?? Really?? He kills his own father in cold blood. (Please note: I cried hysterically at this moment. As far as I'm concerned, it was one of my most devastating deaths in cinematic history.)*

Zack: *Sure, sure, Hans Solo's death is an annihilation of epic proportions— you're*
   watching evil win. It's almost grotesque, and our love for Solo is literally part of our cultural fabric. Excruciating to watch… but part of you hangs on to Kylo. Part of you believes that he could be saved. That maybe under varied circumstances, everything would have been different. Maybe he could be loved instead of hated. I'm just saying he's complicated. Malfoy, you never liked, not even for a second, and you probably never will.

A frog formed in my throat as I wondered if he saw himself that way. Did he think he was a villain who could still be saved? Why? What was so villainous about Zack? As far as I could tell, he was a decent guy. Upstanding. Sure, he was a little stiff, and he was absolutely part of a world that was morally suspect, but he always seemed to do what was right, even if he did it righteously. If anything, he was mostly annoyingly controlled.

Molly: *Fine, Kylo—do you agree to my clandestine meeting, or what?*
   Zack: *Clandestine, huh? Am I your dirty little secret, Molly Mills?*

Was he ever. If my parents knew I was spending my leisure time with a hearing guy, let alone thinking about kissing him, they'd drive up from Florida, stuff me in their station wagon and never let me come back to the northeast. But, whatever, it wasn't like I planned to marry the guy. I just wanted to kiss him. Like a lot. I was still weighing our potential for a fling. Sure, it might end in a blaze of heartbreak—but maybe every girl should date at least one totally inappropriate guy.

Molly: *Oh definitely. I'm pretty sure the rebel alliance would disown me instantly if they catch me with the likes of you, Kylo.*

Zack: *LOL. I'm totally calling Coraline the Rebel Alliance from now on.*

Molly: *Oh no, not that traitor. She is clearly a spy for the Galactic Empire. Always defending your cause.*

Zack: *I knew I liked her. Okay, Rey, what time should I mosey over to the quad?*

He called me Rey. Kylo kinda loved Rey. At the very least, he was infatuated with her. I swallowed back my nerves as I typed.

Molly: *4:30?*

Zack: *Should I bring my keys?*

Molly: *Yep. Be ready to boldly go where you haven't gone before.*

Zack: *Jesus, Rey, pick a consistent sci-fi reference, will ya?*

Twice. He called me Rey, twice.

Molly: *To infinity and beyond.*

Zack: *Oh for Christ's sake.*

Cora knocked on the table to get my attention, and when I looked up, she signed, "You've got a big smile on your face. I take it you have a date this afternoon."

I knew I was gloating—a full-on cat-who-ate-the-canary gloat when I bit my bottom lip and bobbed my head at her.

"Well, guess we better go figure out what you're going to wear."

I furrowed my brow, looked down at my jeans and T-shirt, and then asked her, "Why not this?"

As usual, she rolled her eyes at me like I was absurd. I popped my shoulders and eyebrows at her, physically using my body language to question her motives.

Cora grabbed me by the wrist, pulling me up from the table. Releasing me for just a moment, she emphatically signed, "Tonight you don't want him to be able to stop himself. Tonight, you want to get that kiss."

Then, we were off, her pulling me all the way back to the dorm, driven by the intention to make me absolutely irresistible.

CHAPTER THIRTEEN

ZACK

MOLLY MADE ME FEEL SILLY, and for the first time in my life, I went with it. She said clandestine, and she was going to get it. Donning a black hoodie and black jeans, I approached the main quad cautiously. It was winter, so the sun had already sunk low on the horizon, allowing dusk to rise.

Logically, Molly was standing near the path that led to the parking lots. As soon as I spotted her, I scurried to hide behind a tree. My plan was to make sure she saw me and then run around the quad—shifting from one hiding spot to the next, getting closer and closer to her as I played the spy. But safely behind my first tree, I had to pause and just take in the sight of her.

She wasn't in her regular uniform of jeans and a T-shirt. She was in a dress, a fitted black dress that clung to her hips. She paired said dress with fucking knee-high socks, combat boots and a leather motorcycle jacket. She looked unbearably sexy. Something about the skin showing between the top of her socks and the hem of her dress made me want to see her panties. I wanted to be on the floor, kneeling in front of her, pushing that hem higher and higher. For sure, I had been sending Molly mixed messages, but there was no doubt in my mind that she was trying to unmix them.

This was a date. Plain and simple.

That truth should have made me anxious, but instead it made me giddy.

With my hood up, I leaned half my body out from the tree I'd been hiding behind and started waving my hands around while I drank in her beauty. It took her a minute to notice me, and in the interim, other people eyed me curiously, but most of them wouldn't recognize me. Hoodies weren't really my look. So, I decided not to care if I was seen.

When she finally spotted me, she smiled and lifted her hand to wave. I scolded her for acknowledging my presence by bringing my index finger to my lips. "Shhh."

With her eyes on me, I got low to the ground and scurried so I was behind a bush. Peeking my head out to look at her, I was rewarded with a laugh. From there I went on tiptoe to a tree a little farther away, getting closer to her with each move. Her laughter continued, and by the time I was casually leaning on the tree just to her right, seemingly having nothing and everything to do with her, she signed, "You are very good at clandestine, Mr. Worthington."

I nodded, and then, casually strolling out in front of her, I used my hands to say, "Follow me; I know where we can speak safely."

But Molly didn't play into my ruse. Instead, she caught up to me, and, reaching out to grab my hand, she threaded her fingers through mine. I stopped moving, pulling our joined hands up so they were in front of my face rather than at my side. Everything about having Molly's hand in mine felt right.

Yep, nothing subtle about it. This was a date. Molly Mills was on a date with me.

Letting go of a breath I didn't know I was holding, I brought the back of her hand to my lips and kissed it. Then I strode to my car with her, feeling like a trillion bucks.

She took me to a store for nerds. That was underselling it. She took me to nerd heaven. We had to drive a ways to the kind of mall that clearly used to be the main mall, probably in the 90s or the late 80s, but now there was a better, bigger, fancier mall. So the mall we were in had become a shadow of its former glory, no longer housing the kind of stores you find all over the country. Instead, it was filled with odds and ends, stores that people dreamed up in their living rooms, whole spaces dedicated to selling purple items, or wall clocks, or socks.

Nerd Heaven, which was aptly named "The Grail of the Unsung Hero, Comics and More…," had taken over what used to be a flagship space. In other words, it was a big store, a Sears-size store. They not only sold comics and movies and board games, but they also had events: Magic: the Gathering, casual meet-ups, Dungeons & Dragons leagues, book signings with cartoonists and authors, talks with actors who were in classic sci-fi shows like *Battlestar Galactica.* It was possible that places like "The Grail of the Unsung Hero, Comics and More…" existed all over the world, but I had never been brave enough to look for them or step foot in them, terrified of having my inner geek exposed, but with Molly by my side, I wandered through the aisles, delighted.

I picked up a board game based on Frank Herbert's *Dune* and turned to her, widening my eyes and dropping my jaw, trying to physically make my excitement clear.

Molly laughed and shook her head, smiling. "I guess you like Dune," she signed.

I nodded vigorously, placing the game back on the shelf, even though I wanted to buy it.

"We could buy one," she suggested, her hands moving in a motion that mimicked handing over money to someone, "and play."

No matter how much I wanted one, I didn't think I was brave enough to carry a geeky board game back into my frat house, so I signed, "Not yet, let's look around some more."

From the way her eyes narrowed, I thought maybe she recognized my ploy, but she didn't argue. Instead, we moved away from the board games, getting lost in the rows and rows of comic books.

"Do you read comic books?" she asked.

"I used to." I paused because I wasn't planning on elaborating, but then I did anyway. "My father threw my collection out when I was ten or eleven."

She looked startled. "Why?"

I shrugged. "He said I wasn't a kid anymore."

Her face pinched with dramatic confusion as she dragged the tip of her pointer finger across her palm. "What?

I just shrugged again.

She picked up a copy of *The Walking Dead,* flipped through it and then put it back on the shelf. "He knows comic books are worth money, right?"

I nodded, and then more details just poured out, "He actually burned them. Took me out into the backyard, threw them into a metal garbage can, doused them with lighter fluid and tossed in a match."

Her jaw dropped for a second, but she quickly recovered. "Was he mad? Was it like a punishment for something?"

"Nope," I signed and then shifted my eyes to the comic spines in front of me.

I wasn't totally facing her when I added, "He's just an asshole." I knew she caught what my hands said.

Not wanting to look at her, I kept staring at the comic book, scanning the colored fonts and varied widths, without actually taking in what I was looking at. It occurred to me I'd never admitted to anyone that my father was an ass. I said the words a million times in my head, but I never told them to another soul. I smirked thinking I still hadn't said the words out loud, and then I felt Molly's hand slipping between my arm and my waist, first on one side and then the other, until she had me in a hug, her cheek pressed against my chest.

She was warm and soft, snuggled against my body, and I liked her there. She squeezed, and I squeezed her back. I had the urge to speak, to tell her I liked her in my arms, and even though she couldn't hear me, I couldn't stop the words from coming.

"Sometimes when you're around, I wonder if maybe everything could be different. I like who I am with you. I like who you make me want to be."

I knew she would feel the vibrations of my voice. There was no way she'd miss them. She was literally lying on my breastbone. So when she leaned back and looked up at my chin, I wasn't surprised. She didn't seem to want to let go of me to sign, so she just kind of lifted her shoulders and made a face that questioned what I was saying.

I shook my head casually and scrunched my nose before mouthing less than I felt, "Thank you."

Before we left the store, I got her laughing again. I walked up to one of the guys behind the counter and asked, "What comic would you buy for a girl you liked?"

The dude glanced at Molly, who rolled her eyes at me but also smiled and blushed, so I knew I was on the right track. Turning back to me, he said, "Depends. What is this girl I like into?"

I interpreted his words and mine. "Well, she's a badass who plays the drums and breaks boundaries, but she's also secretly super girly—like she wears pink when no one's looking." I emphasized the sign for "pink" when I was talking, and then when I was finished talking to him, I added a side note in sign only, "Pink not penis, Molly. Gawd."

Next to me she, started giggling.

The dude looked at her and asked, "You like fantasy?" I interpreted. She nodded. "Right. Okay then, I suggest you go with *Sleepless*, man. It's a romantic fantasy about a knight who takes a vow of sleeplessness so he can be ever vigilant over the princess he protects from an assassin."

Sounded good. "Two copies, please."

The guy left us waiting at the register as he ran off to grab the books. And Molly asked me, "Two copies?"

"I want to read it too," I answered.

"Are we starting a book club?" she teased.

"Totally," I snarked, making a face that said, *duh*, before I signed, "It's called the Vinyl Frontier."

In response to that moment of pure genius, she gave me a full-on crackle, complete with snort. And I'm not sure what it was about hearing her make that goofy sound, but I couldn't stop myself. I put my arm around her, pulled her into my armpit, leaned down and gently pressed my lips to hers.

She wasn't expecting it. It wasn't the kind of kiss you saw coming, the kind where you closed your eyes, and time stopped so your lips could slowly drift toward one another. Nope, this was a stolen kiss. The sweet, casual kiss of a man who already thought of her lips as his.

The second it happened, I worried. Panic at my boldness made my grip on her shoulder start to slip, and I thought to release her, but then she pushed up on her tiptoes, tipping her chin and bringing her mouth closer to mine. *Um...can I just say, dude, excellent.*

I lifted my left hand and cradled her cheek, deepening the connection of our lips. Behind the counter, the dude, who had returned, unbeknownst to us, cleared his throat. At that moment, I wished I was like her and couldn't hear him.

We left The Grail of the Unsung Hero, Comics and More... holding hands and each carrying a bag containing our respective copies of *Sleepless*. When we were a few steps from the car, Molly suggested we read the comic the following week over spring break.

"I can text you, and we can talk about it," she suggested.

I agreed. I didn't care that bringing the comic home with me to my parents' house might anger my father. He'd have to find it, and if she was going to text me during the break, then it was worth the risk.

There were six issues in the book I bought us, so I replied, "We'll have to discuss it issue by issue; that means texting every day." As usual, my interest in her made her look away, but she was smiling. I walked her to her side of the car, wanting to be a gentleman. When I leaned in, reaching around her body to grab the handle and open the door for her, Molly stopped me.

She turned so her back was pressed against the door. Lifting her chin, those big doe eyes of hers looked up at me, and for the second time in two days, I found myself captivated by her lips. They were so incredibly perfect. I had the impulse to reach up and touch them again, but before I could, she fearlessly signed, "Kiss me."

Fuck.

Fuck, yes.

I took a deep breath in and tried to do it right. Slowly, I moved my lips toward hers, letting the momentum build, feeling the heat of her breath as I closed in, and then, contact, lips to lips, an explosion of feeling running up and down my spine. Within seconds, there was nothing casual about our second kiss.

Alone in the dark of the parking lot, the beast inside me unfurled. I came at her hard, nudging her mouth open with my tongue, pinning her to my car with my hips. I couldn't stop. Everything about her felt and tasted sweet. And she was so responsive, gripping my lower back, pulling me tighter to her. We were a fury of touches, tongues and teeth.

I relinquished control, letting my desire drive me. I forgot where we were, lost all sight of logic. There was only her and the warmth of her body rutting against mine. My hands slipped down, knowing if I went low enough, I'd find the skin of her bare thighs, and when my fingertips crossed the boundary of her hem, she gasped. It was a desperate, achy whimper that made my dick jump and throb in my jeans. My instinct was to run my hand up her thigh, looking to put pressure where she seemed to need it, but despite whatever she felt, she grabbed my hand and stilled its upward momentum.

I stopped what I was doing immediately and held still, trying to catch my breath and quiet the monster we'd unleashed. It wasn't an easy shift. Everything in me screamed for her. I wanted to make her mine. I wanted no one to ever kiss her but me. I wanted to disappear into the moment—stay forever in the parking lot of some old, dilapidated mall, just us, all lusty and wild.

I lifted my hands to her waist, slowing and gentling my kisses. She followed my lead. When I felt marginally in control, I leaned back and signed, "Sorry."

She shook her head no and then pulled me back, kissing me deeply, tangling her tongue with mine one more time before breaking away and pressing her cheek to my chest. A few minutes later, when we were in our seats in the car, she signed, "That was incredible."

I laughed. "So good, right?"

She bit her lip then hesitantly admitted, "I'm not ready for the rest yet. I don't rush into things. I have to build trust."

"O-K, understood," I signed back, breathing through my feverish need to have my hands on her.

Then, as if it was an afterthought, she added, "I'm not a virgin though."

Hating the idea of her with someone else, I covered my ears.

She shook her head at me and laughed. "You can still see my hands, silly."

"I know," I smirked, "but you told me covering my eyes was rude."

CHAPTER FOURTEEN

MOLLY

I MISSED FLORIDA. I missed the balmy weather and the way the palm trees waved in the sea breeze. I missed my parents. I missed waking up in my house and spending the entire day relating to people I didn't struggle to communicate with. I missed my Deaf friends. I missed their gregarious facial expressions and their snide jokes. I missed the rhythms of their body language. I missed long tables filled with people signing and afternoon BBQs with all the families from the local Deaf club. I missed feeling like I belonged.

So, I was happy to be home.

But I missed Zack.

More than I wanted to.

And the way I ached to talk to him, the attachment I felt, was twisting inside me like a murderous tornado. I felt like a traitor and a liar. Every time someone asked me about school, and I didn't mention him, I was lying. I found myself saying abstract things like, *I love my classes* or *studying music really suits me.* But I couldn't seem to offer any real details because, somehow, he had become intertwined in all of my experiences.

If I talked about my gig and how well it went, I'd have to explain how he helped me settle my nerves. If I talked about Hanover's class, I'd have to mention that he was my interpreter. If I talked about my social life, the highlight was that I was dating a hearing man. Maybe no one would care. But they would talk. They would gossip about Molly, who ran off to music school, and had a new *hearing* boyfriend. My parents would worry.

So, I chose to keep Zack a secret. He was the clandestine man who texted me at night, when I was alone in my bed. His first text came in at eleven pm on the first Saturday of spring break.

Zack: *Good evening! It's two minutes after eleven, and I'd like to call the March 12th meeting of The Vinyl Frontier to order. Roll call, please.*

Even though I'd suggested we discuss *Sleepless,* I wasn't sure he would remember. The week between our date and spring break had been hectic, rife with midterms, and we hadn't really spent a ton of time together—well, not none. There was a study session in the library that went way off course, turning into a full-blown make-out session that ended with me straddling his lap. Thankfully, I wasn't wearing a dress because the hindrance of getting into my jeans provided just enough awkwardness to keep us civilized. After that, we rescheduled our meeting about Hanover's midterm for the more public space of the Bluesy Bean. In general, that meeting had been about studying, although, under the table, Zack crossed his ankle over mine, and he told me I was beautiful three times.

On Friday, the midterm went well. I took my time but still finished early, which I was happy about because I had to finish packing and catch my plane that afternoon. As I'd exited the room, I threw Zack a little wave, but he chased after me, catching my shoulder when I was about halfway down the hall.

I turned to face him, and he grabbed my hand, pulling me into an empty shadowed classroom.

"Did you think you could go without a kiss goodbye?" he asked, his hands moving quickly from signing to pulling me close. He kissed me gently, cupping my face in his hands. Unlike some of the other times we'd kissed, this kiss wasn't about starting a fire between us. It felt like Zack was genuinely kissing me goodbye, telling me with his lips and the slow rolls of his tongue that he cared for me.

At least, I hoped that was what he was trying to relay. I didn't really know. I was, however, totally certain I was struggling to differentiate my growing feelings for him from the reality of his feelings for me. As far as I could tell, our "thing" was still not public knowledge. He hadn't told me to keep us a secret or anything. But he didn't introduce me to his friends or ask me to come by his fraternity.

Also, after he held me to his chest for a good few minutes in that dark classroom, he smirked and signed, "You leave first. We wouldn't want anyone to get the wrong idea."

In the moment, I laughed and kind of felt like he was protecting my reputation, but then later, it felt murkier. Was he protecting me? Or him? I wasn't sure. It was impossible to know how he felt or how he would behave from one minute to the next. As much as I wanted to, I still couldn't trust him with my heart. That said, sitting cross-legged in my bedroom, surrounded by band posters, I was more than happy to get his text.

Zack: *Molly Mills?*
Molly: *Present.*
Zack: *Hey, Rey.*
Molly: *Kylo.*
Zack: *Did you read issue one of* Sleepless?

I did. I read it on the plane. I read all six issues. But I decided to keep that to myself.

Molly: *Yes, I did read it, but before we begin our discussion, can we discuss the nature of The Vinyl Frontier as a book club? My mother's book club includes wine. Is this that kind of a situation, because I am underage, you know?*

Zack: *I didn't peg you for a rule follower—but on my end, this is a wine-less affair.*

Molly: *Arguably, rules are meant to be broken—sometimes. Not all the time. But more importantly, what are you wearing?*

I hit send before I realized how that question sounded, and then I immediately tried to backtrack.

Molly: *OMG.*
Molly: *NOT LIKE THAT.*

Molly: *I am not trying to sext with you. I just wanted to picture you in your surroundings.*
Zack: *I bet you're blushing.*

I certainly was.

Zack: *You look beautiful when you blush.*
Molly: *Thank you. :) So…tell me… What ARE you wearing?*
Zack: *LOL. Nothing sexy. Just lying on my bed in a pair of gray sweatpants.*

Wait, that was a joke, right? He knew that, for a woman, a pair of gray sweats was like the epitome of hotness. There was something about that soft cotton fabric and the way the shadows played on the muted color that showed off just enough of a man's junk to start my furnace. (Most furnaces, I assumed.) Hinting at sexuality was tantalizing.

There was such a thing as too much when it came to looking at boy parts. Deaf people sexted. Everyone probably did, but Deaf people did for sure, and not only had I received dick pics—in the context of my relationship with Jake—but also my friends talked about the dick pics they got from their boyfriends and through online dating. Thing was, I didn't want dick pics. They weren't sexy. Mostly they made me want to laugh.

Penises, just hanging out without abs or heads, or personalities, looked kinda like the alien cousins of mole rats. In context, dicks were very sexy. The way they responded, physically letting you know a man wanted you, the feeling of them in your hand, somehow stiff and hard but still so silky. Mmmm…irresistible. But just a pic? Weird.

Tell me your cock is thick and growing. Tell me you're throbbing. Tell me you wished I could see how hard I made you. Jesus, tell me you're wearing gray sweatpants. That was the way to get me all flushed and flustered.

Molly: *:::Chokes on her sip of water::: Zack!*
Zack: *Just gray sweats….and nothing else. :::smirks innocently:::*

Molly: *I'm going to assume you're not serious and say, volume one of* Sleepless *made me wish he could sleep.*

In the illustrations in the comic, the sleepless knight—Cyrenic—has deep dark circles under his eyes, allowing the reader to immediately see that his magic vow of sleeplessness wreaks havoc on his body and psyche.

Zack: *Right?!? The dude looks exhausted.*
Molly: *But it doesn't stop him from being a badass.*
Zack: *Totally, Cyrenic takes down that assassin in an instant and then keeps vigil over Poppy all night even with an injury. He's a solid hero. I'm into it.*

I was too, but mostly because I knew he was out there reading it with me. It was such a sweet idea.

Molly: *Hey, Zack…*
Zack: *Yes, Mol…*
Molly: *I'm glad we're reading this comic together. I'm happy to talk to you.*
Zack: *Me too.*

I left it at that, knowing *Sleepless* was really just an excuse to chat and feeling a little vulnerable and a lot dreamy about admitting I wanted to hear from him and talk to him over our break.

Twenty minutes later, when I was snug in my bed in the dark, the screen of my phone lit up on my night table.

Zack: *PS. Was totally serious about the gray sweats. Sweet dreams, Molly. :-**

CHAPTER FIFTEEN

ZACK

IT WAS FRIDAY, and I was hiding in the bathroom stall at my parents' country club, trying to decide if I was breaking some unwritten rule if I contacted Molly before our regularly scheduled eleven p.m. meeting of The Vinyl Frontier. It wasn't like we actually scheduled our pre-bed chats over the last week. I just liked routines. And this routine was particularly helpful. It allowed me to know I would talk to Molly every day when I was home but kept me from texting her constantly. I wanted to text her every other minute. I wanted to say good morning and send her little notes throughout the day, but I didn't want to seem like a crazy stalker. And I also didn't want my parents to notice I was texting someone.

Keeping Mol relegated to eleven p.m. made her invisible to them, and that was best. I didn't know how to explain my feelings for her, and, honestly, I was kind of hoping I would never have to. My father had an opinion on and a prescription for all things, and for sure, dating Molly was a thing he would frown upon and most likely deem unacceptable. I was unwilling to face that fate. I didn't want to give her up, but I didn't see how I could avoid it if he knew. So, I decided he would just never know. And yet, I found myself irresponsibly hiding in a bathroom contemplating an end to the routine that kept me in line.

Mostly because my father was a fuck and I was a chicken shit.

Earlier in the week, he mentioned that we were attending a dinner at his club. He was coming straight from the office with my mother and asked if I could pick up the Stewarts, whose car was in the shop. I said yes and thought nothing of it. Only when I got to the Stewarts' house, they were in their car, waving goodbye to their daughter Cecelia, who was under the impression she was not just getting a ride with me but going on a date with the senator's son.

I was furious, like insane in the membrane, smoke coming out of my ears, blow my top angry, but the situation wasn't Cecelia's fault. So, I certainly couldn't take it out on her. Instead, I smiled politely with tight lips and escorted her to dinner, which meant I was both on and not on a date, even though I had no interest in any woman other than Molly.

Sliding into the seat next to my father, I said, "I don't like to be tricked."

He kept his lips wide and smiling as he waved and grinned at the people around him, but his tone was unapologetically stern when he said, "Cecelia is a lovely girl. I was thinking if you two hit it off, I could invite her to join us on reunion weekend."

As an outspoken and successful alum, my father always turned our college's reunion weekend into a family photo shoot slash PR stunt, and I was certain he'd like nothing more than to add her family's clout and money to his dog and pony show.

"I am capable of making my own dates, Father."

He continued to behave as if he were sitting on a float in a parade. "Then why don't you have any?"

We hadn't once made eye contact. We sat side by side speaking through fake, plastered, joyful grins. I sucked in a deep nasal breath before I said, "Right now, dating is not a priority for me. I have law school to chase and the fraternity to manage."

He turned to me and, in a hush, asked, "Are you gay, son?"

He didn't actually think I was gay. He meant to insult me. Gayness was something my father accepted but didn't like. He wasn't the kind of senator who went around attempting to repeal gay marriage, but for him, gay men weren't real men. He was a *prick*.

A part of me just wanted to say, *yes, sir, queer as a three-dollar bill*, even though it wasn't true. I wanted to fight him, but I didn't know how. I couldn't picture myself making a scene surrounded by men and women in fancy clothes, sipping champagne. He raised me to strangle my true feelings, to clamp them down and never give them access to a breath of air, and in his presence, I couldn't seem to behave another way.

So, I said nothing, not a word. I schooled my face, just like him, making my reaction to him invisible to onlookers as he continued to lecture me about the division between who I was and who he expected me to be. It was a lecture I'd heard all my life. He spoke quietly, under his breath, but make no mistake, he was angry. There was no use in answering or arguing. But even as I kept my lips still, my brain couldn't help but retort.

"I am a senator, son. Do you know what that means for you?"

People are watching.

"It means you are being looked at and examined. You are a reflection of me. If you are less than in any way, people will assume that I am not the man I proclaim to be. Do you understand?"

You've told me all of this a thousand times, so if I didn't get it, then I'm a total moron.

"We are American royalty, boy. Dating women of stature is part of your image. It's part of my image. A girl like Cecelia would serve you well."

I almost lost control and rolled my eyes. I was sure that was exactly what Cecelia wanted—*to serve me.*

My father turned to face me and waited a beat, until I felt compelled to look at him. When he was sure he had my undivided attention, he narrowed his eyes and said, "Fuck whomever you like in the dark of night—but in daylight, I expect pretty women of your own stature. If it's not Cecelia, then find someone else. Preferably a lovely young lady who can be on your arm at the reunion. Understood?"

I nodded and choked back everything I felt. The words "or what?" felt seared on my tongue. What would happen if I didn't follow his rules? Would he disown me? Would he discredit the people I cared about? My father's threats were always unsaid and undefined. He controlled me with the mere insinuation of horrifying consequences.

Eventually, he turned his attention from me to shake the hand of a golf buddy. I stood and made my way out of the ballroom, down the hall to the men's restroom, and then I shut myself in a tiny white room that was more toilet than anything else and stared at my phone, desperate to speak to the one person who made me feel real.

Finally, after listening to the sound of other people flushing for ten minutes, I gave in. I wanted Molly. I wanted the way she made me feel and the taste of her sweet mouth. I needed her.

· · ·

Zack: *I wish I could kiss you right now.*

She didn't answer right away. But I stayed put, waiting, hoping I'd hear from her. I dropped my head against the wall behind me and looked at the ceiling. It was pocked with those little textured bumps, and my mind focused on them, looking for recognizable shapes, like I did gazing at the clouds when I was a kid. I didn't know how much time had passed, but it wasn't a minute.

Molly: This meeting of the Vinyl Frontier is unexpected. (But welcome.) If you kissed me
   right now, where would I be?
   Zack: In the men's room at my parents' country club.
   Molly: Please tell me you're not sitting on the pot sending me smexy senti-
ments. Ew.
   Zack: LOL, no. (Gross, btw, but also, would I tell you if I was?) I'm not, really! I'm leaning against the wall, trying to ignore the pot.
   Molly: You're hiding.

Her understanding of my behavior didn't make her a genius. People didn't usually hang in toilet stalls alone, but still, I was impressed she assessed the situation so quickly.

Zack: Maybe.
   Molly: From whom or what do you hide, pray tell?
   Zack: Did we just fall down a wormhole and land in a Shakespearean play?
   Molly: Cute. But obviously an attempt to ignore the actual question.
   Zack: Fair. But I don't really want to talk about it. Is it okay if I just say I'm having a bad night?

The ellipsis appeared and disappeared a few times. I wondered what she was thinking. Hiding in the bathroom wasn't the best feeling, and there were certainly people who would think me weak. Would Molly?

I felt like I was such a mess in front of her, always making mistakes and being moody or needy. And yet, she still seemed interested. Despite my nonsense, she asked me out on a date, took me to a place she thought I would like, actually listened when I told her my secrets and was concerned about my feelings. I wanted to always offer her the same. Maybe I could. Maybe Vos was right. Maybe I could make her happy.

Molly: I wish I was kissing you too.

Molly: I wish we were hiding in that bathroom because you wanted to press my back against that wall and make me tremble. Tease and touch me with your mouth and hands until I begged.

Over the last week, we'd joked about sexting. I'd sent her innuendos. Said things that made it clear I fantasized about her, but they were hints, shadows of my thoughts, nothing this forward. I wondered, why now? But, also, her sexy words settled like a gift. The nastiness of my father's judgment and perceptions faded behind the surge of my own lust. She distracted me from my melancholy with her desire. I read and reread her words, getting hard behind the zipper of my khakis.

Zack: Fuck, Molly. Now I'm locked in a toilet, hard as fucking nails and grinning like an

idiot.

Molly: I miss your mouth. I can't stop thinking about it. Do you want to know what I think

about, Zack?

Zack: Yes. Jesus, yes. But where are you? 'Cause if you say anything else, I'm gonna have to take my dick in my hand. It's so hard right now, it's throbbing. And, call me crazy, but I don't want to masturbate while you're sitting at your parents' dinner table.

Molly: I, too, find myself hiding in a bathroom, my bathroom.

Zack: Leaning against a wall?

Molly: A sink vanity.

Zack: Better. I could lift you up onto that.

Molly: Mmmm… and then what?

I'd never done anything like this before, and I wasn't certain what to say. Everything I knew about sexting and talking dirty came from the media. In the movies, after asking a woman what she was wearing, men said things like, *my cock is so hard for you right now* and *s*pread *your legs and touch your pussy for me, baby.*

Don't get me wrong. If she'd let me, I'd watch that—on repeat. Fuck. But saying something like that felt disingenuous. Sure, the words might be sexy, but anyone could say that to her. Sexting with Molly felt important. It was personal. I didn't just want to get off. I wanted to get off with her. I wanted this to be about us. So, rather than just talk dirty, I told her what I thought when I thought about her.

Zack: *I think about your panties. I think about that dress you wore the night we first kissed. I think about crouching down on my knees, running my hands up the outside of your thighs, pushing up the hem and catching my first glimpse of pretty pink lace.*

I sent the text and then reached down, gripped my hard length through the fabric of my pants and squeezed. There was an ensuing groan. I couldn't contain it. I'd never been so turned on in my life. Nervous that someone might have heard me, I stilled, listening to the silence, wondering if I was actually going to follow through and make myself come. I didn't know if I could do it quietly.

Molly: *I can see you here. Kneeling before me. My heart is racing. My thighs are shaking. I want you to touch me, Zack. I want to feel the drag of your fingertips over the edge of that lace.*

Zack: *Can you do that for me, Molly? Drag your fingertips over the elastic of your panties and pretend it's me?*

· · ·

There was a pause. A minute or two where there were no texts from her, and there was no ellipsis either. Anxiety bloomed at the edges of my thoughts as I wondered if asking her to touch herself was too much, but then I received an audio file. Odd. Not sure what to expect, I lowered the volume and brought the speaker to my ear.

It was a short file. Only a second long. One sound. A moan. I assumed it was the sound she made when she pretended her fingers were mine. It was incredible. The sound vibrated my eardrum like a gong, sending rhythmic vibrations straight to my balls. Molly couldn't hear, but somehow she knew her sounds made me crazy.

I couldn't stop myself. I unbuttoned my pants, pushed my hand inside my underwear and gripped my cock, pinching the tip, trying to keep myself from coming right then and there. I wanted more. I wanted to hear her come.

Zack: *I'm teasing you now. I'm still above your panties, stroking your lips and grazing*
   your clit so lightly. I want you like you said, so worked up and trembling that you have to
   beg. I want you desperate and shaking, and then I want you to slip two fingers under the
   fabric and tell me what you find.

CHAPTER SIXTEEN

MOLLY

I WASN'T in the bathroom. I was sitting on the couch in my parents' living room, which was separated from the kitchen by a breakfast bar, supposedly watching closed-captioned television, while my mom cooked dinner behind me. And suddenly my conversation with Zack was getting awkward. I wasn't sure why I lied to him. Probably because I needed to console him. I wanted to grab his attention, pull him from whatever ugliness his parents put him through, and remind him that I thought he was cool no matter what movies he liked or what job he grew up to pursue.

I'd figured it would just be a goofy sexy exchange. In the past, I'd found sexting was more about the dude. My ex, Jake, would say something raunchy that mostly made me laugh, and then I would say some things back that made him come. Honestly, I'd never even touched myself texting dirty with Jake. It was all pretend.

Ridiculous, I know, but Jake's idea of what words turned a woman on was laughable. Once, out of the blue, he sent me a text that said, *I wanna fuck. So bad.* Not *Baby, if you were here right now, I'd lay you down and fuck you,* or even *I want to fuck you so bad.* Nope, no need to specify that he wanted me. He just *wanna fuck.* Way to make a girl feel special, right? He also used the word "cock" a lot: *touch my cock, suck my cock, shove my cock, rock my cock, slam my cock. Here a cock, there a cock, everywhere a cock, cock.* But even still, I liked that he wanted to play. I liked thinking about how to turn him on. Sexting felt creative to me. It pushed me to consider what I wanted and desired, and it made me feel like I knew what men wanted and desired. I liked to turn a man on; that felt powerful.

So, when I texted Zack from the living room couch, I wasn't thinking I'd get turned on. I was thinking I'd turn him on. Up until that moment, our late-night meetings of The Vinyl Frontier were PG-13—intimate but not overtly sexual, but Zack always signed off by hinting he was thinking of me in a sexy way or that he wanted me thinking of him that way. And I was. I couldn't stop thinking about making out with him.

It was almost like the more we didn't talk about what it felt like to finally kiss and touch, the hungrier I got for more of him. In bed at night, I fantasized about him. I thought about his strong hands pressing into the sensitive flesh of my breasts, circling my nipples, and his mouth working on my neck and the rut of his hips against my core. I thought about watching him pull his shirt over his head, and then the press of him against me, skin to skin. I dreamed of touching him, stroking him or sucking him. I was so worked up about him and genuinely nervous that when we returned to school, there would be no stopping me from doing something stupid.

But when I got that text from him, at an impromptu time—telling me he wanted to kiss me—it felt intimate. Even more so once he admitted he was struggling. It wasn't a casual text. In an off moment, I was where he turned. I was the person he reached out to. It was a perfect storm of intimacy, hot broken sad boy needs you, wants you, and you want him too. Kaboom! Lightning blasts a smoking black hole in the protective wall around your heart, and you find yourself asking if he wants to know the ways you fantasize about his mouth.

Only, unlike Jake, Zack wasn't a *I wanna fuck* kind of a guy. He didn't want to play a game of *cock me here; cock me there; cock me, cock me everywhere.* No, he wanted to say seriously erotic things to me about me. Sexting with him felt more intimate than actually having sex with Jake. There was no way I could finish the conversation with Zack sitting on the living room couch.

I stood, pocketed my phone and crossed through the kitchen, trying to avoid making eye contact with my mom. She was bustling about, back and forth from the fridge to the counter, pulling out ingredients. Not looking at her caused more harm than good. Holding a tomato in one hand, she grabbed my arm just before I got out of the room.

I turned and, tucking the tomato in her armpit, she signed, "Come help me chop."

"I have to pee," I lied.

She smirked. "Who were you talking to so intently?"

Ugh, annoying. Why did she always have hawk eyes? My whole life, I'd made the mistake of assuming she wasn't paying attention when she was lurking.

"A friend from school."

"A guy?" She was teasing and smiling, but then her face fell. "Wait…"

I could see the gears spinning. It was occurring to her that if I was talking to a guy, he most likely wasn't a Deaf guy.

I diverted her attention by bouncing my feet and repeating, "I have to pee."

With a tight, awkward smile and a forced laugh, she threw up her hands and then signed, "By all means, pee."

I didn't lie to my mom. We didn't always agree, but we discussed things, so as I walked down the narrow hall to the bathroom we all shared, I felt creepy. But that creepy slither in my gut didn't stop me.

Safely behind the locked bathroom door, I pulled my phone back out of my pocket and reread Zack's texts. His words made me press my thighs together. Zack mentioned when we made out in the library that the sounds I made turned him on, which was why I sent him a sound. But I'd faked the first sound, and I didn't want to fake the second one. Leaning against the sink vanity, my back to the mirror, I unsnapped the button on my jeans. My mother wasn't going to open the door when she thought I was using the bathroom, and she wouldn't hear that I was doing otherwise, but still, the scandalousness of touching myself in the bathroom—pretending it was Zack—had me double-checking the door lock. I cupped my hand over my panties, applying pressure everywhere and nowhere. I was already turned on, the fabric damp.

Zack: *Too much?*

I liked that he was nervous and conscious of my response. With the hand that wasn't in my pants, I hit the record button and brought the speaker to my lips as I used the other hand to tease myself. Doing as he asked, I strived for delayed gratification, tickling along the edges, groping over the fabric until I couldn't bear it anymore. Then, I captured the sound that escaped as I slipped under the hem of my panties and pressed down on my most sensitive flesh. I hit send on the file and then typed.

. . .

Molly: *It would be better if it were really you. But at the thought of you, I am wet and*

shaking. Should I make myself come, Zack? Do you want to hear it?

Zack: *:::gulp::: Yes, but fair warning, if you do that, you may obliterate what control I*

have left in your presence.

Molly: *Will you come with me? I want you to. I want to think of you locked in that cubicle stroking as I come.*

I read my own words, and they felt unfamiliar and a little scary. Being intimate with Zack brought something to the surface I never felt before. I hungered for him. I was raw and dirty and desperate around him. I wanted him boldly, in a way that forgot to be careful. I would die if he showed these texts to other people. But I didn't think he would. I trusted him not to.

Zack: *I'm not trying to offend, and I hope I don't, but I wish you could hear me too because I don't have the words to tell you how fucking turned on I am. Everything I try to type feels too raunchy and graphic for how I feel at this moment. But, yes, I'm going to come with you, thinking of you, dying to touch and taste and smell you. I'm going to make a fucking mess and sounds other people might hear because I can't help myself. I need this with you. And later, I'm going to read this and listen to the sound of you and do it again, dreaming of the reality. I'm enthralled with you, Molly Mills, and I don't want it to stop.*

I came, leaning against the vanity, with my own fingers in my panties. Zack wasn't even in the same state as me, but I was pretty certain we'd just had sex for the first time.

After my bathroom escapade, coming out and taking my seat at the dinner table felt awkward. I was giddy, flying high on the uber sexy, heart-pounding, oh-my-god-did-that-just-happen feelings, so making eye contact with my dad was a hard no. And my mom, very clearly, had more questions about who I was texting prior to my whiny demand, "Just let me go so I can spend fifteen minutes locked in the bathroom peeing."

So, dinner with my parents was… quiet. Meaning, there was a lot of "Can you please pass the potatoes?" and not a whole lot else. My parents were chatty people. They talked about everything. I was pretty sure my mother could tell you how my father felt about everything from NASCAR to the Florida gubernatorial election, not because she knew him so well after twenty-three years of marriage, but because they had discussed their feelings about all things in detail. They expected that level of communication from me. Nothing was private in our house. There were no secrets. We didn't have to agree, but we discussed.

Honestly, their level of transparency was pretty normal in the Deaf culture. Deaf people gossiped a lot, and they were often very blunt about their feelings. If they thought you'd gained weight or gotten a bad haircut, they weren't going to pretend otherwise. Deaf people expected the truth from other deaf folks. It seemed odd or nasty to those in the hearing world, but in our culture, the truth was never nasty. It was honest. When the world was stacked against you, you counted on honesty from those who loved you most. Like most Deaf people, I learned to alter what I understood as typical and acceptable conversation and comments so I could converse in hearing society, but the expectation was that, at home with my deaf loved ones, honesty and transparency would prevail.

It wasn't, and they knew it, so I was getting the cold shoulder, or if you will, the silent treatment. And the truth was, I deserved it. By not telling them about Zack, I was lying. Zack wasn't a fling. Even if he dragged me through the mud and broke my heart into a million pieces, what was between us wasn't casual, and I knew it. Piece by tiny piece, I was trusting him with my heart. Not telling my parents about that was wrong.

I put my fork down and took a deep breath before I brought my fist to my chest and signed, "I'm sorry."

My mother stilled. My father kept eating but rolled his eyes to show he was annoyed.

To confirm, my mother moved her hands before her, stating, "You are dating a hearing boy."

I nodded.

"Is he kind?" she asked.

I nodded again.

"Does he sign?"

I smiled. "Yes, but he makes hilarious mistakes."

"Like what?" my father asked.

"He confuses words: taco and stop, pink and penis, meet and sex."

My mother smiled a little sad smile, but still a smile, and my father smirked before signing, "The usual suspects."

I nodded. And then, looking at the softness of their faces, a well of sadness filled the space behind my breastbone, and suddenly I was crying. I punched my chest, emphatically saying, "I am so sorry. I know this isn't what you want for me."

My mother crossed from their side of the table and came to sit next to me. Putting her arms around me and pulling me to her chest, she started to rock us in her arms like I was a baby.

My father signed, "Don't cry. It's okay."

"I want to make you proud," I signed, smashed in my mom's arms.

My father grinned. "Done."

Pulling away from my mom, I leaned back in my chair to say the next part. "I don't know what I'm doing. It's hard to be brave all the time, and when I'm with him, it's like being here, like I belong."

"I think I will like him," my mother signed.

I sniffled, and then I laughed. "You would," I told her. "He's very handsome."

My father, who had gone back to eating at this point, retaliated with, "Oh, gross, I can't stand him already."

Later, when I was getting ready for bed, my mother came into my room. She was in her nightgown, a lavender oversized sleep shirt printed with a giant gray kitty head and the slogan, *I'm ready for my cat nap.* I'd been expecting her. There was no way my mother would just accept a relationship with a hearing man, not without some warning.

She ushered me to the bed, and we sat cross-legged, facing each other, like girls at a sleepover. She looked at me for a beat, lifted her hand and brushed the hair out of my eyes. I expected her to say something along the lines of *be careful*, but instead she signed, "Before your father, I fell in love with a hearing man."

I was shocked. I also realized that, in all the times my mother spoke of deaf women being mistreated in relationships, she never actually told me anything about the relationships she had before my dad.

"His name was Henry," she signed. "And I was crazy about him." She shook her head and shifted her eyes away, blushing like a girl.

"Did he sign?" I teased her by calling back to the question she asked me at dinner.

She nodded and added, "And he was kind. But his family wasn't. They didn't want him to be with a deaf woman."

I looked down at my lap. I knew what she was trying to say. Even if Zack and I adored each other, the deck was stacked against us. She reached for my chin and tipped my face up so I was looking her in the eye.

"I would love him again," she signed. "It hurt, but it was worth it."

I quirked my head at her. "Really?"

"Don't get me wrong. Your father is my number one love, but each relationship in our lives teaches us something about ourselves. They add layers, make us bigger. And while I feel protective of you and want to scream and yell that this choice could blow up in your face, I can't know that. I don't have a crystal ball. And I certainly don't want to keep you from experiencing things because I'm afraid for you."

"But, Mom, what if it ends badly?" I asked, feeling like I knew full well that it was going to.

She sighed, and then, with chagrin on her face, she signed, "Most relationships that end, end badly; otherwise, they wouldn't end." She took my hand in hers, holding it, looking at it and then looking back at me. "You have always been brave, baby. Just enjoy it. If it ends, you will have learned something, and there will be another, I promise."

***

The following day, I left Florida feeling peaceful. Having everything out in the open with my parents just felt right, and after my discussion with my mom, I decided to stop trying to control whatever was happening between Zack and me. What would be would be.

Cora picked me up at the airport. She was one of those rare people who parked the car and waited in the terminal. I told her that wasn't necessary. But then, through the glass wall that separated the gates from the baggage claim, I saw her and couldn't help but feel overjoyed. Her blond frizzy curls bounced as she jumped up and down, bursting with excitement at my arrival, and it occurred to me that I was home. I had two homes. I belonged and was loved in both places. I wasn't exactly sure when I acclimated to loving school and thinking I belonged, but it had happened.

On the walk to the car, Cora dragged my bag, and I confessed that Zack and I had been texting over the break. She knew about our date. She helped plan it. And she knew he'd kissed me, but I'd honestly been way more tightlipped about my connection with Zack than Cora deserved me to be. Seeming to catch on that something in me had shifted, she had a million questions and kept having to pause to let go of my bag to ask them. After three stops, she suggested she ask them all at once, and I could answer them at will.

"Okay," she took a dramatic breath, as if she were preparing for a race, and then with lightning speed and the agility of a ballet dancer, she signed, "are you two like an item now? Is this a relationship or something more casual? What do you mean you've been texting over break? Texting or sexting? And if the answer is sexting—do tell."

She wagged her eyebrows and then continued her assault, "Can he still be your TA if you bang him? Are you going to bang him? Clearly, he's hot, but what does Zack Worthington talk about? Golf? The end of communism? Is he funny? Finally, and most importantly, do you think he has a friend for me?"

I laughed. I wasn't sure about Zack, but Cora was definitely funny. Smiling happily at her, I signed, "I missed you."

"Ditto. Like a million times over. I'm so glad you're home." She grabbed the suitcase again and then looped her other arm through mine. We started heading for the car park again.

Signing lopsided because we were arm in arm, I said, "Honestly, Cora, as much as I'm enjoying the love, I can't answer your questions when we're linked like bosom buddies."

She let go of the suitcase one final time to say, "Screw it, I've waited this long. Hoes before bros. Let's go eat. You can answer all my questions over Ethiopian food."

I laughed. "You know I have to use my hands to eat that, right?"

She rolled her eyes at me. "Don't act like that's not true of all food, dude."

CHAPTER SEVENTEEN

ZACK

IT WAS A TRADITION. On the returning Sunday after any break, the officers of my fraternity went out for dinner together, and not for burgers. We always tried someplace new. Somewhere we'd never been before, at least not together. The goal was to act like civilized beings for a change.

The post-break get-togethers were my favorite fraternity dinners of the year. First of all, only the top fifteen brothers were present, so it wasn't a chaotic scene of noise and clatter, and, secondly, the guys actually hung out and chatted, rather than slamming beers and talking smack about women. Except Dickie, he was still a burping, farting boisterous asshole, but in the past, I'd made sure he and I were at different ends of the table, and he didn't seem to notice.

Anyway, this time, I let Vos pick the restaurant and manage the reservation. He chose an Ethiopian restaurant called Queen of Sheba. Growing up in and out of DC, I was exposed to some of the best Ethiopian food in the country and developed a hankering for it, so I was pleased with his choice.

Even from the parking lot, I could see the atmosphere of Queen of Sheba did not disappoint. There were burgundy shades framing the windows and hammered metal lamps hanging from the ceiling on brown cords, spilling a warm shower of golden light over the patrons and booths. Eager for the explosion of cardamom, cinnamon and black pepper on my tongue, I complimented Vos as we waited for the others to gather before going in.

"Good choice. Love Ethiopian food."

"You have no idea. Wait till you taste the injera," he tossed out a chef's kiss and added, "so fluffy…so spongy…sooo good."

I couldn't help but smile. "As it should be, but if I remember correctly, the assignment was someplace you hadn't been."

"Was it?" Vos asked cheekily. "I could have sworn you said someplace you hadn't been."

Skulking in our direction from his BMW, Dickie called out, "Do we really have to eat this slop, Prez?"

Before I could check myself, my eyes rolled at his idiocy, which was arguably bordering on racism, and I snapped, "Not at all. If you'd like to wait out here, I won't complain."

Next to me Vos chuckled, and one of the other guys bantered, "Oooooo, Dick face, Prez just grew a pair and put you in your place."

In an attempt to make my comment more joke and less annoyance, I added, "Not to worry, Matthews. I am sure they have a children's menu."

Dickie smirked. "Hey, Prez, fuck you."

"A terrifying offer," Vos chided under his breath.

I just shook my head before circling the beasts. "Okay, assholes, we are on our best behavior tonight. Remember—this is us out in the community, representing our house."

"Aye, aye, Captain," Dickie clamored, slapping his feet together to stand at attention and salute, poorly, of course.

I didn't respond. I just turned and headed for the door to the restaurant. Inside, there was a lovely smiling woman behind the counter.

Even though I could see the large table in the back set for fifteen, I said, "We have a reservation."

With a continued smile and thick accent, adding an "eh" sound before the word *should*, the woman kindly answered, "I should hope so."

Grabbing a stack of menus, she turned to lead us through the restaurant, and that was when I saw her. Molly.

I stopped short, my breath catching in my throat. In my head, I pictured what I would do if I were free for five seconds. I knew my stride, heavy fast steps in her direction. I felt the bend of my body as I slipped into the seat next to her, pushing my hip against her hip, resting my hand on her thigh. I heard her giggle as I brazenly grabbed a swath of injera from the basket on the table and sopped up a taste of the doro wat the two women were sharing as I said, "What's happening, ladies?"

Only I didn't do any of that; I just stood there dumfounded as Vos practically walked into my back. Molly looked happy, sitting at a corner table with Coraline. They were laughing and talking. I wondered what they were discussing, and I thought to myself, if I had a few seconds to watch, I could definitely eavesdrop on their conversation. But I didn't have a few seconds.

Behind me, Dickie asked, much too loudly, "Hey, Prez, isn't that your deaf charity case?"

Coraline turned immediately.

I swallowed before clenching my teeth, hoping if I stayed strong, I could keep the walls around me from falling in.

As usual, Vos jumped in, "Jesus, you're an asshole."

"What?" Dickie teased, trying for innocence as he whined, "She can't hear me."

There was the rumble of laughter as a few guys added to his nonsense.

My nostrils went wide, and I clenched my fists. I wanted to maul him. I wanted to throw him to the ground and spit in his face. But my father's training held. My throat narrowed, and my breathing grew tight. It was like I didn't know how to act on the things I truly felt, like I was trapped in a cage, keeping up appearances whether I wanted to or not.

Cora stared at me. Her nostrils flared as she waited for me to respond, waited for me to be bold, better than I was. My Adam's apple bobbed as I swallowed down my guilt. I wanted to be better. I wanted to scold Dickie. I wanted to absolutely put him in his place, and I would have, but even if I did, I still couldn't greet Molly the way I should. I could not walk over there, pull her into my arms and tell her how happy I was to see her.

If I did, they would all know how I felt about her. They would see it in the way I lost control, the way I grinned and stared, the goofy lovesick look she brought to the surface, and there was no honor among beasts. Before I even got back to campus, the whispers would begin, and before long, my father would call asking about Molly.

Defeated, I tried to calm Cora with my eyes, but it was no use. With pursed lips, she tapped Molly and pointed in my direction as she signed "Z-A-C-K." Everything slowed as Molly turned to look at me. The light in her eyes was so genuine. The smile she threw me was bright and wide, and I felt like it might shatter my heart.

Sternly, I said, "Her name is Molly. And she is not a charity case, Dickie. She is a lovely woman." Then, stepping to the side, I pointed to our table, trying to usher my brothers in that direction. One by one, they stepped past me.

Across the room, Molly's smile fell. She gave me a little tentative wave, and I tipped my chin at her, not knowing how to relay the situation to her without losing ground. As my brothers passed, they were generally silent, but of course Dickie had something to say.

Elbowing me in the side, he chided, "I think she has a little crush, boss. You should tap that."

I didn't take my eyes off Molly's. I held her gaze and begged her to see what I really wanted, how I wished I was jumping over the tables to pull her into my arms. Risking everything, I brought my hands up and signed, "Please, forgive me."

Her brow furrowed, and she shook her head slightly before turning back to Cora like I wasn't there at all.

Within minutes of taking my seat at the table with my brothers, Coraline and Molly paid their bill, stood and left. She never looked at me again, not once. I knew I should have acted differently, but I didn't know how. I had to talk to her. Explain the situation. As soon as I was out of the restaurant, I tried texting.

Zack: *Please let me explain.*

No answer.

Zack: *That was not about you. You are wonderful.*

Still no answer.

Zack: *Please, Molly.*

. . .

Nothing. We had made a plan to have breakfast at the Bluesy Bean in the morning, but I couldn't wait till then. I drove directly to her dorm, parked the car and lingered outside the door of the building until some schmo appeared and took no issue with letting me sneak in behind him. I definitely needed to rant to the Dean about the fact that the key cards were only as secure as the idiots who owned them, but at that moment, I was get-down-on-my-knees-and-pray thankful that most people functioned like sweet, unsuspecting sheep.

I wandered up and down the institutional hallways with commercial-grade blue carpet, white walls and wooden doors decorated by their inhabitants, searching for some sign of her. I didn't know what room Molly was in, so I just roamed, hoping I could find her. At first I thought maybe there would be something on a whiteboard that gave her away—her name or something related to drumming or a cut-out of a hand shaped in an ASL symbol perhaps? But, ultimately, I identified her room because, unlike anyone else, she had a doorbell. Molly couldn't hear a knock. She needed the lights to flash in her room to know someone was at her door. Obviously, the school had provided that accommodation for her.

Taking a deep breath, I pushed the button. I listened for movement behind the door. Nothing. It hadn't occurred to me that she might not be there. I pressed the bell a second time, watching the shadows shift at my feet as lights flashed on the inside. She wasn't there. Unwilling to give up, I pressed my back to the wall next to her door and took a seat. I could wait. Even if she was gone all night, I could wait.

CHAPTER EIGHTEEN

MOLLY

I STAYED in Cora's room. She held me while I cried. I felt so stupid, so naive. I thought we were building something. I thought he was different. I told my parents about him, and he didn't even have the balls to introduce me to his friends. Cora kept noting that he had the decency to look upset about it and to immediately ask for forgiveness, but I couldn't be some guy's deaf secret. I wasn't ashamed of being Deaf, and Zack wasn't going to make me feel otherwise.

Eventually, both Cora and I fell asleep, but when the sun rose, I was up again, and I wanted a shower. I wanted to feel fresh, wash away the sorrow and the salt of my tears. After jotting a little thank you note for Cora, I grabbed my suitcase and left quietly. We lived in the same dorm. Cora on the sixth floor, me on the third.

On a Monday morning at five a.m., a college dorm is like a morgue, eerily dead. There was no movement in the hallways whatsoever. Because of my bag, I took the elevator. Usually, I favored the stairs. They were closer to my room.

I still felt stunned that Zack practically ignored me, but I also felt thankful that it imploded before I did something really stupid. That was what I was telling myself as I focused on maneuvering the wheels of my bag over the carpet to my room, which was why I didn't see him until I was just a few feet away.

With his hands tucked prayer-like under his cheek, he curled in the fetal position on the floor in front of my dorm room. Before my brain registered annoyance, I wondered how long he'd been lying there and had the instinct to go inside and get a blanket to cover him up. His khakis and baby blue oxford shirt were wrinkled, but they were the same ones he'd been wearing in the Ethiopian restaurant. Even in his sleep, he looked focused, like he should be accomplishing something. He had to be cold and uncomfortable.

I wanted to take care of him, but then I remembered how he stood there and didn't even wave. How he treated me like I was dirt, something nasty and embarrassing that he had to keep hidden from his friends. I also knew there was a lot that Zack kept hidden, and, in his case, being something hidden didn't have to mean he didn't care, but, still, it didn't work. It couldn't.

I thought about just stepping over him but decided I didn't want to be inside knowing he was still lying in the hall. I wanted him gone. I didn't particularly feel like being close to him, so rather than crouch down and shake him awake, I kicked him, right in the shin. Hard.

He grabbed where my foot hit and most likely spurted a profanity before remembering where he was and jumping up to stand before me with a serious set of p-p-p-lease-forgive-puppy-dog eyes. Nope.

Curtly, I signed, "Can you loiter elsewhere?"

He ignored my question, diving right into his own defense. "I don't give two shits what any of those guys think, Mol. You are so much better than any of them. That wasn't about you. I was dying to leap over the table and smash you to my chest, but my world is all about…"

He faltered, probably because he didn't know how to explain to me that being seen with the Deaf girl would ruin his carefully crafted persona.

"Go on," I egged. "Tell me that your friends wouldn't understand your interest in me—that caring about me, wanting me, it's…" I shifted my hands back and forth, pretending to be Lady Justice weighing concepts. "Embarrassing."

His eyes heated, and his nostrils flared. Furious, he signed, "You are not embarrassing. If any one of those fuckers thinks that, they can kiss my ass and eat my fist."

I took a small step backwards, surprised by the genuine vitriol he was spewing. He believed what he was saying. He wasn't even vaguely embarrassed of me.

Gentler, I signed, "Why didn't you come over and say hello, Zack?"

He sighed, looking longingly down the hall like he wanted to grab my hand and make a run for it. When he looked back, he signed, "Molly, I'm so fucking sorry. Most of my brothers are real assholes, but none of them, none, even begin to compare to my dad. And if those boys knew how I feel about you, my dad would find out, and he would ruin it. Somehow he would make your life or mine a living nightmare until we gave up. He always ruins things for me. He poisons everything to ensure I have no choice but to stay on the path he's ordained. I didn't introduce you or treat you the way I wanted to because I cannot lose you. I cannot let my father know you exist. I cannot let him take you away from me, and I still haven't figured out how to make sure that doesn't happen."

I didn't want to believe him. I didn't want to trust him. The whole night felt smarmy. But I didn't doubt for a second that he was telling his truth. Exhausted, I took out my keys and opened the door to my room before I said, "You are not a child. You don't have to do what he says. You could just walk away."

Zack attempted a smile but couldn't seem to make that happen. I pulled my suitcase past him, dragging it into the room, and then I turned back his direction and signed, "I'm upset. I don't feel ready to forgive you, and I'm not sure I can."

He nodded, leaning his head against the door frame, watching me, sort of dopey, smiling to himself. I stared at him, hoping I was giving off an I-need-a-whole-lot-of-space-from-you vibe. But he didn't get the message, or maybe he did, and he refused to accept it, staying put, watching me like I was a work of art he needed to memorize. After an unruly amount of time, he lifted his head, and the bold and cocky version of Zack—the one who inserted himself as my interpreter and sent me saucy text messages—was back.

"I think you'll forgive me, Molly Mills." He moved his hands slowly, a sexy smirk on his face.

I bit back a smile. Dammit. Trying to seem snooty, I signed, "Oh, really?"

He nodded. "I'm persistent, and you like that."

"Do I?" I asked before turning to drop my purse on my desk.

He waited till I was facing him again to sign, "You're already starting to melt. I can see it in your eyes."

"I am not." I shook my head in annoyance and then pointed to the hall. "I think it's time for you to go."

Before he closed the door, he goofy-grinned at me and signed, "Next Friday, we're going to go out. You, me, Cora and my friend Vos. By then, all of this will be forgotten, not because it should be, but because, between now and then, I'm gonna make damn sure you know that I know how important you are to me."

———

Monday 11:30 a.m.

When she woke, Cora came to find me. I'd showered and was unpacking, but mostly I was trying not to get lost in thinking about Zack and the choices he made. Cora was oddly delighted to hear I found Zack sleeping on my stoop.

"Did he have a good explanation?" she asked.

Abandoning my unpacking, I sat down on my bed and signed, "Not really, but sort of…" I was still confused about how to process Zack's take on his world and how that affected me.

"It doesn't make sense that he's embarrassed of your deafness," Cora signed, leaning on my desk. "I mean, in the restaurant, I thought that at first too, but he looked too sorrowful. That boy is crazy about you, I think. He's just trapped in his own issues. He has been since day one."

I knew she was right, but I would never do what he did to him. Still, I wasn't sure I really understood what it was like to be him. My parents had expectations for me, but mostly they wanted my happiness. I could talk to them. Trust them. Feel safe with them. Whereas, Zack's father seemed to see Zack as a vessel for or a reflection of his success as a man and a senator. Zack felt judged, controlled, and tortured by him. I couldn't imagine what that was like. But I also wasn't sure I wanted to be part of Zack's mess.

"You're right. I know you are," I signed, flopping backwards, making signing difficult but still possible. "But, Cora, do I really need to be there for a man who doesn't know how to integrate me into his life? A man who can't stand up for what he wants and needs?"

With her arm out like a scarecrow and her elbow bent, Cora pushed the palm of her hand back, sort of waving it, signing "Not yet," and then, seemingly exasperated, she flopped next to me. "He can't stand up for what he wants and needs yet."

I sighed, and we lay there next to each other for a few minutes just being still, surrounded by my conundrum. Eventually, Cora sat up, and I followed suit.

"Your phone is buzzing," she signed, getting up to cross the room and grab it off my dresser.

As she was walking back, I told her, "He wants to go out on Friday. You, me, him and his friend Vos."

Cora grinned and handed me my phone. "Like a double date?"

Ignoring her question, I signed, "We shouldn't go, right?"

She laughed at me. "No, we are going. I'm not letting your drama keep me from meeting my own hot frat boy."

I shook my head at her and looked down at the text message I received.

Zack: *I've told you this before, but you are brave, Molly. Braver than most. When I look around me at people our age, they are all hiding. (Myself included). Hiding from what they want, trying to fit in. You are the opposite. You're running headfirst at your dreams. Incredible.*

I read it twice and then glanced up at Cora, feeling overwhelmed.

"I guess that is something good." She smiled. I handed her the phone and let her read the message. Handing it back, she signed, "We are so going on Friday, but you go ahead and pretend we're not."

"Should I say anything back?"

"Nope," she signed with an evil grin. "Let him stew today. He should suffer some."

"What about tomorrow?"

"That's your call, lady."

I didn't know what to say, so for days, I just let him text me.

Monday 5 p.m.

Zack: *From the first moment I saw you, I couldn't look away. You are so incredibly beautiful. But your beauty isn't like a picture in a magazine. It's bigger, more dynamic. It's not just bones and flesh. It's heart and soul. Sometimes, I think I conjured you or that you were conjured to possess me—force me to see the value in being touched by beauty.*

Tuesday 7 a.m.

Zack: *I'm drinking coffee at the Bluesy Bean without you. It sucks. I miss your face.*

. . .

Tuesday 9:30 a.m.

Zack: Did you cut Hanover's class because of me? I'm sorry if I've made your life harder. On Thursday, bring Cora. I promise not to bother you.

Tuesday Noon

Zack: I'm not going to lie. I hate that you're not responding. But I deserve it. You should never feel sad because of me. Never.

Tuesday 10 p.m.

Zack: Have you ever seen the film Passengers? *It's a love story. Sort of. It takes place in the future, and all these people are put into stasis, so they can travel aboard a spaceship to a new home. The journey is light years—it would take lifetimes. They only survive it because of suspended animation. Only one guy wakes up 90 years too early, and he's alone. He's so alone. So he does the unthinkable. He wakes a woman. He lies, makes her think she just woke up like him, but eventually she finds out. He's basically stolen her life. But they're trapped on a spaceship together for eternity. They fall in love. I think I'm this kind of hero, Mol. A selfish one.*

Tuesday 10:30 p.m.

Zack: It is possible that I am a little drunk. Fine. A lot drunk.

Wednesday 12:01 a.m.

Zack: I don't want to be the selfish hero or the villain with feelings. I want to be fucking

Jean-Luc Picard or Harry Potter or Superman. I want to be good. I've always wanted to be good. What do you say, Mol? Can I be your sleepless knight? Can I take a vow to protect you and treasure you, even if I can't have you?

. . .

Wednesday 2 a.m.

Zack: *I shouldn't tell you this. I should focus on wooing you, convincing you I am worth forgiving, but, Molly, I listened to the sound of you tonight, and I want to drown in it. I can't imagine a life where your pleasure isn't mine. I'll die.*

Wednesday 11 a.m.

Zack: *Jesus, fuck. I am doing a shit job, aren't I? I am always a god damn fool with you. I tell you things I should keep to myself. I don't do that with anyone else. Is there like a hacker or some tech geek I can call to eradicate the texts I sent last night? Forgive me.*

This was the moment. He was apologizing for his truth again, and I couldn't let him. I adored the Zack who was fighting to be good, the Zack who wanted to be better than the ugliness he came from. I liked when he let his walls down and showed his true self. This Zack, the one in turmoil, fighting to be a better man, he was mine.

Molly: *I do not give you permission to delete them. They are mine.*

The ellipsis dots appeared and disappeared.

Zack: *"Ever have that feeling where you're not sure if you're awake or dreaming?"*

Because he put the words in quotation marks, I copied them and googled the quote. *The Matrix.* God, he was literally an encyclopedia of sci-fi and fantasy references. I was pretty sure that one look at his internet history and Netflix queue would reveal his true nerdiness to anyone wanting to look. It also wasn't lost on me that stories about other worlds were an awfully powerful escape for a boy whose life wasn't fun. My heart hurt for him.

· · ·

Molly: You're awake, Neo. Now, go on, leave me alone.
    Zack: "As you wish."

That one I knew: the devoted farmhand from *The Princess Bride.*

Wednesday 5 p.m.
    Zack: No need to reply. One of the guys was just listening to Paul McCart-
ney's "Maybe
    I'm Amazed," and, well, Mol—you are with me all the time. I'm carrying you
and the
    magic you've created in my life. Forgive me, please.

Thursday 8 a.m.
    Zack: Will I see you in class?
    Molly: Yes.

CHAPTER NINETEEN

ZACK

I GOT HER COFFEE, even though I was pretty sure she would already have one. I just couldn't show up empty-handed, and I didn't know what else to bring. If I brought flowers or chocolates, I would create a spectacle, and Hanover would get annoyed. I also brought her a pastry in a brown paper bag, a sweet sugary cronut thing I thought she would like.

Even though she had eventually responded to my texts and sort of admitted to liking my words and sentiments, I had no idea how she was going to react to me in person, and I was terrified. I changed my clothes three times and called Vos up to my room to check if I stunk because I was so nervous, I was sweating.

I got to the classroom early. I wasn't sure if she was coming with Cora or alone, but, hopeful, I took my regular seat near the front of the class, preparing to function as her interpreter. Molly arrived on time, leaving us no room to talk before class began, but Cora wasn't with her, and I took that as a positive sign. Wanting her to see that I knew she valued doing well in Hanover's class, I was all business. But I couldn't help but steal glances at her face. She was wearing a bit of makeup, lip gloss and mascara, making her eyes pop and her lips enticing. I'd seen Molly with makeup a handful of times, but not usually in the morning for class, and if I had to bet, that was Cora's doing.

She looked soft and beautiful, bewitching. I wanted to touch her so badly. I wanted to kiss her. I couldn't fathom I'd gotten through the week without seeing her. But, somehow, I managed to hold myself back and do my job like the gentleman I wanted to be. When class was over, she started to gather her things, but I couldn't let her go without saying something.

"Molly," I signed. "Please stay a moment and talk to me."

She slowed, shifting her weight, taking her time putting her things away. The room got emptier and emptier, and soon it was just us and Hanover, who already had his bag on his shoulder and was preparing to leave too.

He addressed me, "Is everything okay over there?"

I nodded and signed as I spoke so she could know what was happening. "Yes, sir. Just a couple of things to go over from Tuesday's class. Is it okay if we sit here a while?"

He smiled. "Of course. Although, I'm pretty sure Ms. Mills is just as competent as you are, Mr. Worthington."

I interpreted as he spoke, delighting in the way he made Molly grin, before I replied, "Probably more so."

Hanover gave me a knowing look, and then, as he exited the room, he sort of grumbled, "They always are."

Once he was gone, Molly sat back in her seat and turned to face me. I just stared at her, forlorn, wanting it all to go away, to just be back in the place where I was crazy about her and she trusted me.

"Are we going out tomorrow?" I asked.

She nodded yes.

"Does that mean I am forgiven?"

She shrugged.

"I'm going to do better."

She shrugged again.

"Will you say something to me?"

She shook her head no.

I swallowed, absolutely shattered that I hurt her, and I still wasn't sure how to stop it from happening again, but I hoped I could. I sighed and, then, removing my hand from her knee, I stood. "I understand." I signed, "Tomorrow we'll have fun. Okay? And then we will take it slowly from there."

I was nodding like an idiot, as if I needed to convince myself. Molly stood too. I tilted my head down to look into her eyes and, surprising me, she reached up and caressed my jaw. The sensation of her hand on my skin reverberated down my spine, making me feel weak. I steadied myself by grabbing the table next to us.

Molly smiled a small sad smile, and then she pressed up onto her tiptoes and gently kissed me. It was a tiny quick kiss, just the flutter of her lips like the passing wings of a butterfly. But as soon as it happened, everything inside me went calm. Even if she couldn't say it. She forgave me. Her lips were just the salve that reminded me Molly liked me for me. I didn't have to be anyone else to make her happy. I was still looking at her face when she dropped back down to flat feet and went to turn away from me. I didn't let her.

Wrapping my arms around her waist, I grabbed her and kissed her with my fucking soul. I poured every ounce of feeling in my heart into the collision of our lips, desperate for her. She didn't flinch or withdraw. She accepted my offering, kissing me with as much passion as I was giving. Unlike the times we'd kissed before, this wasn't a sex kiss. It wasn't a grope-y, hungry, pull-at-your-clothes kiss. This kiss was a message. It was a love letter. I wanted her to understand that, even if we didn't make it, she was it for me. I was going to carry Molly Mills in my heart for the rest of my life.

Releasing her, I took a step back and watched her hand drift up and touch her mouth. Looking stunned, she ran her fingers over her lips as if they were unfamiliar, like she didn't know they could feel the way they felt right then.

I signed, "I am yours, Molly. I can't lie to you, I might fuck it up. I probably will. But you own me." Then, I picked up my bag, smiled at her contentedly and casually added, "See you tomorrow."

She managed to nod, and then I left her there.

CHAPTER TWENTY

MOLLY

WE SAW A MOVIE. Deaf people go to the movies, and most theaters have accommodations—they have a variety of different devices that provide captions. There are mirrors you put in your cup holder that reflect captions projected on the back wall of the theater. There are tiny LED screens you can hold that provide captions. There are also these weird fandangled smart glasses that attach to a box you wear around your neck that are totally uncomfortable. None of the choices are great. But we saw a movie with captions on the screen, and it wasn't a foreign film.

When we got to the theater, I said something to Cora about coming with me to the desk to talk to the attendant so I could figure out what accommodations they had for me, but Zack interrupted my conversation by signing, "You don't need it."

I furrowed my brow at him. "How will I know what the characters are saying?"

He smirked. "You'll read the captions on the screen."

I looked to Cora, thinking maybe I missed something, or he signed something wrong, but she just shrugged and signed, "Apparently, there are captions on this film."

And there were. In a theater full of hearing people, I watched a film with open captions on the screen. It was delightful. As if for once the world acknowledged that I existed and that people like me existed and that something as simple as writing the words the actors were saying on the bottom of the screen utterly included a deaf person in everyday life.

After the movie, Zack asked me what we wanted to eat, and I said burgers. So, we went to Kate's Kitchen, a fairly typical diner with good greasy food. Cora and Vos sat on one side of the booth, and Zack and I squished into the other side. Trying to distract myself from how much I liked the feeling of his thick, muscular thigh pressed against mine, I started talking about the captions.

"I just can't believe they have captions on the films there. How did I not know that?"

Vos, who obviously couldn't sign, said something, and Cora quirked her head at him, clearly confused. She signed, "What do you mean 'they don't'?"

I felt Zack's legs shift. And then Vos made a pained face and started talking. Next to him, Cora translated, "Zack made that happen. He called there, set it up and paid for it."

I turned to look at Zack, who was scolding Vos. He wasn't signing, so I hit him in the arm.

He swallowed and looked at me.

"Sign," I was emphatic with my demand.

He kept his eyes locked on mine as he spoke to Vos but signed for me. "Dude, I didn't want her to know that."

"Why not?" I asked. It was a thoughtful thing to do. I was glad he'd done it.

He swallowed. "Because it wasn't a ploy for your affection. I didn't want you to think I did it to get in your good graces. I just wanted you to have a good night. I did it because it should be that way."

Well, it might not have been a ploy for my affections, but that right there had my insides melting. He was going to be the death of me. Trying to hold it together, I gave him one curt nod and then turned, signing to Vos and Cora when I said, "It should."

Cora interpreted for me. And Vos nodded at the sentiment.

"So," Cora said, dramatically drawing out the word and the sign, while making a face that clearly showed the awkwardness of the moment, "Vos, you're the stranger here. Tell us about yourself."

Looking to me and then to Cora, Vos asked her, "Will you make sure Molly understands what I'm saying?"

She already had been, but I liked that he wanted to make sure I was included.

Cora signed, "Already on it, dude."

Under the table, Zack slipped his hand into my lap and squeezed my thigh. The warmth of his palm penetrated my jeans and made me feel shivery.

Across the table, Vos said, "I'm from Texas. My dad is a rancher, which is great, but I'd be more than happy to never ride another horse in my life." We all laughed. Vos was genuine. It was a rare quality. Turning to Cora, he said, "You're a stranger to me too, Cora. What's your story?"

Cora shrugged. "Grew up in New York. My brother is deaf. My mom's a rabbi. I like bagels and pizza."

"You have great hair," I added.

Zack interpreted for me, and Cora blushed.

Vos nodded at Cora, and then he reached up and absent-mindedly fingered one of her springy blond curls. She side-eyed him, leaning away, physically relaying the question, *what are you doing, man?*

As if woken from a reverie, Vos snapped his hand back and looked like he was apologizing. For obvious reasons, Cora wasn't interpreting anymore.

Turning to Zack, I signed, "That was odd."

He replied, "Maybe he's into her."

"Maybe he was hypnotized by her hair."

Zack laughed, and then, looking down to smile at me, he signed, "You are adorable, Molly Mills, and I'm so happy to be sitting next to you."

I buried my face in his shoulder for a second before coming back up for air. I admitted, "Me too."

The rest of the meal was uneventful; we ate burgers and French fries, and we laughed a lot. Vos apologized to Cora at least fifteen times, and Zack kept his arm slung over my shoulder. Being next to him felt normal, like it was where I belonged. The guys split the check even though we argued to pay our share. We piled into the car and drove back to campus.

Zack parked in a main parking lot that was closer to my and Cora's dorm, even though the walk back to the fraternity house for Vos and him would be longer. Slowly, the four of us strolled through the campus, Vos and Cora walking ahead of Zack and me.

"Despite his strange obsession with Cora's hair, I like Vos," I signed.

"I like you," Zack replied, making me giggle. Then, seriously, he added, "I don't want tonight to end."

I didn't either.

He looked uncomfortable, pained even as he signed, "Shit, Molly, forgive me if this sounds fucking creepy or makes you think I only want to get into your pants. But will you stay with me tonight? I promise, I'm not asking you to have sex with me. Absolutely nothing will happen if you don't want it to. I just want to be with you."

I wanted to be with him too.

CHAPTER TWENTY-ONE

ZACK

I MARCHED her through my frat house like she belonged there. A growing bold part of me wanted everyone I knew to see her on my arm. I fully intended to introduce her to anyone whose path we crossed, only we didn't cross anyone's path.

When Molly announced to Cora that she was going with me, Vos offered to walk Cora home, so we were literally standing in the living room of my frat, completely alone.

"Is it normally so quiet?" Molly asked me.

"No," I signed. "I don't know where they are. A lot of the guys go out on Friday nights, but it's not usually this quiet."

She didn't seem convinced. I hated that she was thinking I brought her home, knowing I still wouldn't have to introduce her to anyone. Trying to shift that situation, I plopped down on the couch and signed, "Let's sit here till they get back."

She shook her head.

"Really. I want to sit here and wait for someone to come home so you can see I'm going to be different."

Grabbing my hand, she pulled me up. "Show me your room," she signed.

I lived on the third floor in the largest room in the house. A lot of the house was gross, but my room wasn't. I kept it neat and clean. I painted the walls a gray-blue. I had an antique wood queen-size bed that I bought at a tag sale freshman year, and a brown leather sectional I'd acquired in a similar manner. I intentionally cultivated a space that was masculine and elegant, very British monarchy, because when people were in my room, I wanted to be understood as a leader.

Molly didn't say anything when we entered the room. She wandered around slowly, touching my things. I closed the door behind me and leaned against it, watching her roam. She examined it all, tested the bed, fingered the books on the bookcase, hit the spacebar on my computer, disengaging the screen saver. I let her do as she pleased because everything was as I liked it. Tidy. There was nothing she couldn't touch or see.

After exploring for a bit, she opened the closet door and started to poke around, looking on the top shelf, crouching down to check the back corners. Her behavior was bizarre. I got her attention by flicking the light switch next to me.

Scrunching my nose at her and sort of laughing, I used my hands to ask, "What are you doing?"

She shook her head at me, baffled. "Is there nothing here that you love?"

I stared at her, wanting to tell her, wanting to shout that the only thing I'd ever loved was standing right in front of me.

"Where are your copies of *Harry Potter*? Or your ratty old *Star Wars* t-shirt that you only sleep in?" She crossed the room and pulled open my desk drawer. "There has to be a *Star Trek* transmitter in here or something."

She knew there was nothing. Coming to stand next to her, I leaned on the desk, watching her shuffle through the paper clips and pushpins. I signed, "I cannot have any of that."

"But you love it," she signed aggressively. "Why can't you have just one token?"

"Because he took them all," I signed matter-of-factly. "And if I buy new ones, he'll take those too."

"It's nuts," she signed. "Why would someone care what kind of stories you like? So many people love *Star Wars,* Marvel and *Star Trek.*"

Expressing my father's perspective, I signed, "Common people, regular people. Soft people who worship idealism over rational thinking and power."

"So, he thinks liking the good guys makes you weak."

I nodded.

Shifting so she was standing in front of me, she signed, "You are not Kylo or Draco, Zack. You're not Superman either. You're just a man. Sometimes you're going to do the right thing, and sometimes you're going to screw up. That's normal."

Objectively, I knew she was right. But I didn't feel that truth under my skin. Deep down I was still certain I would never be better than my father, and that would always mean I was a villain. Still, I signed, "I don't want to screw up with you anymore."

"I know." She glanced away.

I reached up and stopped the movement of her chin, gently turning her head back to face me. "Can I tell you what I feel, Molly? Or will it spoil things?"

She didn't let me speak. Instead, she kissed me.

CHAPTER TWENTY-TWO

MOLLY

THERE WAS no circling around it. I wanted him. I was also pretty sure that before the semester was over, our relationship would crumble one way or another. But even if that happened, I didn't want to protect my heart. My mother was right; the risk and the experience were worth it. So, no more talking. No heavy words or sappy sentiments. It was time to speak with my body. Bodies were more truthful than words. It was time to show him how much I felt, how much I wanted.

I kissed him with every intention of letting the kiss be the key that threw open Pandora's box. It was a wild kiss. It wasn't sweet, soft lips. It wasn't a gentle, hesitant tongue. It was a fire kiss. It was a bossy, bold, open-mouth, hungry kiss. I pushed my hands into his hair and crushed my body against his. His hands swiftly gripped and pulled at my waist, his fingers pressing into the flesh of my hips.

Our kisses were like a fever, inducing delirium. Everything but the heat and rhythm of his labored breaths slipped away. We were a blur of moving lips, sloping necks, ticklish earlobes and angular collarbones. Everything blurred. Like all there was in the world was the slick pass of his tongue on my skin, firing up nerves and synapses. I drifted in a haze, my own breathing heavy all around me.

He slipped a hand under the hem of my t-shirt, pushing it up, and the trail of his thumb over my ribs made me shudder. He slowed the movement, tracing his thumb in reverse, eliciting a second shudder and an instinctual sound. Goosebumps blistered in the wake of his touch.

Forgetting his original intent, he turned us so I was leaning against the desk, and then he dropped down, wanting to toy with the sensitive patch of skin he'd discovered. I took the initiative to remove my own shirt as he dragged his tongue over the path his thumb had traced. The sensation was like a shower of glitter, sparkles of pleasure, rippling under my skin.

As he kissed his way over my torso and hips, it occurred to me that maybe I didn't really know about sex. I knew about orgasms. I knew about perfunctory movements: kiss me, press against me, touch my breasts, slip between my legs, rut and rub until we come. But I didn't know about this kind of worship. I didn't know what it felt like to have a man drunk on my skin, possessed with an unyielding need to please every inch. It was like I was learning about my body with him, like he was teaching me how I wanted to be loved.

I wanted us naked. I wanted to explore him the way he was exploring me. I unsnapped my own bra, revealing my breasts. My nipples were already puckered, but they pebbled more as soon as they were bared to the air. I looked down as he looked up, leaning back to take in what I was offering, his eyes glazed and dreamlike. My breasts were small, less than a handful. In the ninth grade when they seemed to stop growing, I prayed puberty would hit again, doubling their size. But in this moment when he looked up and mouthed, "Perfect," I knew they were.

High on his knees, he drew a small, slow circle around one nipple and then the next. My hands found his thick hair, gripping, holding on, and he drew my peaks into his mouth, sending undulating ropes of pleasure up and down my spine. Again, he didn't seem frantic. He repeated every touch I responded to again and again, seeming to feed on the pleasure he was bringing.

Eventually, I begged for the bed. First, by unconsciously signing "B-E-D" with my fingers, which made me laugh at myself.

My giggles got his attention, and he leaned back, smiling in a way that seemed very self-satisfied as he used his magic hands to ask, "What's so funny?"

"I want to get off this desk and get in your bed," I signed.

"That's not funny." He grinned at me as he signed, "That's fucking amazing."

I pushed off the desk, moving around him before stopping and turning my back to the bed. In my absence, he stood so we were separated but facing each other. He watched as I slipped out of my jeans, and then, in nothing but my panties, I signed, "You have a lot of clothes on."

"You don't," he joked, but his hands moved to the buttons of his oxford. He held my gaze as he slipped each of the shiny white circles through their tiny holes, revealing more and more of him. We always talk about women's bodies as beautiful; lush curves get compared to flowers and jewels, but as the planes of Zack's chest became visible to me for the first time, I was stunned by the elegance of him. He was lithe and strong, possessing the long, fierce muscles of a thoroughbred, built to endure.

My tongue ached to trace every line, to dampen every crevice. I wanted to know him, memorize him, discover all the secrets his body had to reveal. As I watched, he continued to remove his clothes methodically, draping them over the desk chair.

"Better?" he asked once we were both in our underwear.

I shrugged, teasingly biting my lip before sliding my panties to the floor.

His pupils flared, and something in his demeanor shifted. Keeping his eyes locked on mine, the part of him that was eerily intense and almost stoic flared as he signed, "If you are offering it all, I will take it, Molly. I want to know you from the inside more than I want to see the sun rise. But I need you to be clear right now. I need to know your boundaries, your needs. I want us to communicate now, before I get lost in the dreamscape that is you naked and seemingly willing in my bed."

The air that I was somehow still pulling and pushing in and out of my lungs felt spiked, like I was getting high just from breathing. Every inch of my body felt swollen and achy. He was mere feet from me, and I missed the rough press of his hands and the sweet scrawl of his mouth. I didn't want it to stop. I needed him.

But his gesture slowed and gripped my racing heart. He was asking for my consent. It was a strangely formal and elegant way to be. He was also unearthing his underlying fear, a possible loss of control when it came to me, like my naked body brought forth something within him that he wasn't sure he could trust, something unbridled. I could see it, the restraint he was already exerting, the tension in his neck and shoulders, the tightness in his expression, and it fed me, heightening my desire. But more than that, this moment was to ensure that what we were communicating with our bodies was what I wanted. This moment was for me, specifically because, in the dark, under the covers, the language we used to communicate would become complicated.

I knew, everyone knew, that spoken words were a large part of sex in the hearing world. Deaf kids see hearing porn. The internet exists. We watch it with captions on and see the varied sexy, sweet and raunchy things that hearing partners say to each other in the throes of passion. Obviously, communication with your partner is always part of sex, especially decent sex. There is instruction, encouragement and connection in the language partners exchange.

Many deaf people talk to each other in the dark—holding hands while signing so we can approximate what signs are being used, or if they know it, they can use Pro-tactile ASL, which is a language developed for the DeafBlind based on touch. Or sometimes with a lover, you develop your own shorthand, but this was the kind of thing that a hearing man wouldn't know.

For Zack and me, there wouldn't be instant access to language while having sex. We didn't have a shorthand or a formal system in place. So, rather than traipse through it in the dark, he was standing before me making sure the most important details were clear from the get-go. And there was a beauty in that, a grace.

I didn't realize I had any lingering apprehension, but I did. Some scared part of me laid down her fear that I was not a notch on his belt. I felt seen. I felt wanted. I felt the man before me was invested in connecting to me. The sex we were about to have was important to him, as it was to me.

I lifted my hands and signed, "I want you. I want to feel you hard and thick between my legs." At my words, his eyes fluttered closed. I had more to say, so I waited for them to reopen as he drew in a series of deep breaths. "You will be able to tell what pleases me. You already know that. You will feel me shudder and hear my breathing race, and the sounds you elicit with your touch. Your body will tell me things as well, and tonight, that will suffice, but moving forward, we can find a way to communicate that isn't sign—a shorthand of touches that speak volumes, only to us."

The formality of his desire slipped away as he pushed his hand through his hair, obviously muttering the word, "Fuck," and then, as if he couldn't stop himself, he reached down and squeezed his hard length through the fabric of his boxer briefs. Pleasure crossed his face, and I felt my core tighten at the sight.

Curious, I teased, "Did what I say turn you on, or just, like, the promise of sex with me in general?"

Releasing his dick from his grip, he signed, "Hell yes that turned me on. There was talk of sex together multiple times, my cock between your thighs, shuddering, you wanting to please me and a secret sex language." He winked.

"Honestly, you're lucky I didn't just cum in my shorts." This was the man I adored. The one that was all business one minute and awkwardly goofy and honest the next.

Echoing his silly tone, I teased, "Well then, why are you still way over there? And more importantly, when are you gonna lose the shorts?"

"Now," he signed, right before he turned off the overhead lights. He left the tiny lamp on his desk aglow, and, illuminated by mellow golden shine, he dropped his boxers so they pooled at his feet. I could have stared, taken my time and really looked at him, but as soon as he was fully naked, he was moving, closing the distance between us. The collision of his skin with mine was like nothing I'd ever felt before. It was like a blinding flash of pleasure, followed by a low-grade buzz that didn't stop. The only thing I could compare it to was the way my joints vibrated after a perfect gig. Only it wasn't my limbs; it was my whole being.

My body sparked and hummed. Everything slowed. Flashes of skin. My fingertips running up the thickness of his thigh. The flutter of his lips tickling the sensitive flesh behind my knees. The slow, soft tangle of our tongues. His teeth scraping gently across my shoulder blade. The velvet length of him in my hand. The slide and slip of his fingers through the wetness between my legs, A constant ebbing and flowing current of pleasure all around, endless and every-where. Making love to Zack was like music. It was like breathing the heartbeat of an entire rhythm section. With him I became the music I adored.

It shouldn't have been that way. The first time with someone was supposed to feel awkward. It was supposed to be unfamiliar. A new lover's body was an alien instrument. It had to be deciphered and then practiced. That was reality. But Zack and I were something else. It was like the learning process was so deli-ciously intoxicating that we never wanted it to end.

We kissed and touched and tickled for hours, never quite reaching release. It was an unspoken pact. We were on a journey of discovery, committed to letting the pleasure build and coil but never actually end.

As a teen, I'd seen a documentary about people who had out-of-body experi-ences, and I'd laughed. There was something too woo-woo about the idea for me to take it seriously, but on that bed in Zack's room, I got it. I felt utterly connected and detached at the same time. My body became a vessel of incredible reactions, bowing and bending to his touch. It was exactly the feeling that people revere, the feeling they write love poems about. When the pleasure becomes so fuzzy, so blurred that you can no longer tell the difference between his enjoyment and your own.

In the end, when he finally donned a condom and slid his girth inside me, I clenched immediately. We were sweaty and luminous, and my body took him like I was where he belonged.

CHAPTER TWENTY-THREE

ZACK

WHEN I WOKE UP, she was asleep in my arms, the velvet nakedness curled around me. Heaven. Heaven with a raging hard-on. I tried to convince myself to be a gentleman, to let her sleep and just listen to the quiet mumbles of her breath moving in and out of her lungs, but my hands had a mind of their own, gently tickling their way over the landscape of her skin, wanting the feeling of every inch.

And then my tiny movements elicited responses. First, a trail of goose bumps in my wake. Then, a smattering of tiny needy sounds, little gasps and moans, and, finally, the shifting of her legs and the adjustment of her hips so she pressed the side of her warm pussy to my thigh.

For Christ's sake, I was not a saint.

Laying her on her back, I kissed my way down her torso. I spent hours the night before learning exactly what pleased her and made her tremble. I'd run my fingers over every part, dipped into every crevice. In all aspects of my life, I'd always been meticulous, studied every detail, learned all the angles. Before Molly, sex was biological, focused on the release. But with her, my needs felt secondary. I wanted her pleasure. Pleasing her drove me insane. It was this exquisite feedback loop. The more I pleased her, the more intense my own feelings and sensations were.

Which was why I dragged my tongue down past her belly button slowly, savoring the faintly salty flavor of her skin. Gently, I nestled my torso between her legs, spreading them, making room for my shoulders. She stayed relaxed, awake and aroused but still flirting with the powdery edges of her dreams. When I was nestled in the cocoon of her thighs, I blew a slow, steady stream of warm air against her swollen lips, and she shivered, dropping her knees wide, showing me the smooth wet pink flesh of her pussy, and I was lost.

I dove in like a starved man, wild and relentless. I roughly dragged the flat of my tongue up and over her most sensitive flesh, hungry for the cries I induced. I circled and sucked. I stroked and fingered. I slid my hands under her ass cheeks, digging my fingers into the flesh, pulling her tight around my face because it wasn't enough.

Nothing with Molly was enough. I wanted more. I wanted to crawl inside her. I wanted to be part of her. I wanted her to come so hard that I left a mark, an unforgettable stain on her soul. I didn't know if that was possible, but I wanted it to be true.

She didn't disappoint. She came loudly, forcefully, shattering on my tongue, her fingers knotted in my hair, pulling herself tighter against my mouth. She came with her thighs clamped around my face. She came wildly, making me want to sit up and band my fists against my torso like a silverback gorilla.

Molly made me feel bold. She made me feel driven. She made me want to be bigger and better and more real. Touching her only magnified that feeling.

When she released her thighs, I looked up from my perch, and she grinned at me. It was a rebellious smile. The kind that screams "I love trouble."

Mischief in her eyes, she signed, "I've been seduced and satiated by Superman. Now, show me the dark side. Fuck me."

Her words plowed through the last vestiges of gentlemanly refinement, leaving behind only the beast. Giving in to the desperation to devour her, I sat up, and in one move, fast and hard, I flipped her over, grabbed her waist and drove her into the bed, burying myself deep inside her.

She cried out beneath me, her hips bucking, her back bowing. She was wet and swollen from the pleasure I gave her with my mouth. I growled out the immediate intensity of knowing her bare. Buried to the hilt, my cock throbbed. It fucking pulsed with desperation. I wanted to rut. I wanted to drive myself hard inside her over and over again. I'd never been raw inside anyone.

I worried I'd gone too far. I didn't think about what I was doing, I just acted. Took what I wanted. I couldn't remember another time in my life when I'd been so obnoxiously bold and reckless, and the fear that gripped me was staggering.

I was afraid I hurt her, that I pushed past an unspoken boundary. I stilled. Took a breath and tried to find control, but the animal under my skin continued to rage. *She asked for the dark side. She wanted villainous.*

Unconsciously giving in to my instincts, I pulled my hips back, slowly dragging my cock from her depths. She chased me. Pressing up on all fours, she looked back over her shoulder. Her eyes were wide, frenzied and sparkling. She bit her lip. She was waiting on me. She wanted to be fucked. And by some miracle, it was my job.

So, I plowed. I held tight onto her hips and drove into her body again and again until I felt her clamp down all around me. As she came, I held on and prayed. Prayed I could hold out. Prayed I could stay inside her until she was done. Prayed I would get to come surrounded by her warmth, and then, when she was a mess of tiny shudders, I pulled out and exploded all over her back. It was a fucking mess. The best mess I ever saw.

The beast satiated, I jumped up and grabbed a folded towel off the top of my dresser. Still panting, she pressed her ass against my hand as I wiped her clean, and then she collapsed, flat on her belly, turning her face to the side so she could look at me.

`"Are you hungry?" I signed, high on the thrill of her, and with her scent in my nose. "Let's go to breakfast." I was so drunk on her that I thought I might be brave enough to traipse her downstairs into the kitchen and make her goddamn eggs while my brothers gawked.

She smiled at me, lazy and languid post-orgasm.

"I don't want to get up," she teased, and then she stretched in my bed, pulling the sheet up between her legs and covering the majority of her body while still leaving one leg and one curved ass cheek exposed. "I'm going back to bed," she smarted before tucking her hands under her cheek and closing her eyes.

Fuck. She was so beautiful. I wanted to fight her, push her to get up, let me show her off, prove to her that I was going to keep her, but she looked so incredibly peaceful that I just couldn't.

"Fine," I signed dramatically, even though she had her eyes closed. "Twist my arm and make me spend the day in bed with a fucking punk goddess."

A tiny smile played at the edges of her lips. Was she laughing at me?

Narrowing my eyes, I peered at her, creeping closer to see if her eyes were actually open. When I was right upon her, she busted out laughing.

"Could you see me?" I signed, laughing with her.

She nodded, pulling me down into the bed. "My eyes weren't totally closed."

"That shit was creepy." I laughed, getting twisted up in the sheets with her as she wrapped her arms around me.

She shrugged and then broke away to say, "Trick from childhood," before nestling into my armpit. Unbelievably happy, perhaps as happy as I'd ever been in my entire life, I fell asleep for a second time with her in my arms.

"Zack!" someone hollered, followed by three solid pounds on my door. I stirred groggily, wanting to stay asleep next to the warmth of her body. But the noise continued.

Another screech, "Zack!"

My eyelids lifted, taken aback by the light filtering in through the window that was making the dust in the air visible.

"One of you must have a key." I knew the sternness in the man's tone.

"No, sir. Zack is the only one with a key to everyone's room." That was Vos, and what he was saying wasn't true. He had the skeleton key to everyone's rooms too. My mind raced trying to shake off the weight of my sleep and decipher who was at my door. "Perhaps we should try calling again, Senator."

Vos said the word *senator* a little too loudly. He wanted me to hear it. He was talking to my father. Another slam. "Son, are you in there?"

Fuck. Fuck. Fuck.

Trying to buy time with confusion, I sat up and called out, "What the hell?"

Not caring what his answer was, I started shaking Mol. She was heavy with sleep, warm and peaceful against me, unable to hear his incessant knocking. At my touch, she sighed, scooching back, pressing tighter against me. Her dark hair fell like feathers against my chest.

For a moment, I imagined opening the door, my dick swinging in the breeze, and telling my father to fuck right off. But he'd see her in my bed. If he saw her, he'd begin his plotting. One glimpse would be all the ammunition he needed. His lip would curl, and he would fire. He'd say something ugly, and the war would begin.

My father was a controlling narcissist. Every move was about spinning his story. Every choice the people around him made was either a peace offering or an attack. So, if I wanted to stay in his good graces and have access to his money and his power, then I accepted the role he assigned to me. Up until Molly, I was willing to accept the situation. Sure, it was uncomfortable but required, kind of like wearing a suit jacket to an outdoor wedding in July, every day for my entire life. When it came to Molly, I would not let him devise the yarn. He would never shape her story. Never.

I knew at that moment, listening to him beat on my door like an alpha gorilla, that the only way to protect Molly was to walk away from him. To stand up to him. To be who he didn't want me to be, my own man. Still, I couldn't make that happen immediately. I needed time, a plan. I needed to attack. Make it clear there was no going back, that if he attacked Mol, I would fight back. I couldn't make that happen in the safe space of my fraternity house, where breakdowns, blowups, mistakes were easily buried and silenced behind a cloak of brotherhood. I had to stand up for myself in a public sphere—make a show of my betrayal, so he couldn't pretend it didn't happen.

There was no choice. I shook Molly again, and when she still didn't really stir, I jumped up and started grabbing her clothes and throwing them in my closet. I also pulled on a pair of sweats. While my attempts to wake her had little to no effect, my leaving the bed had her sitting up and rubbing her eyes.

Shrouded in my sheets, she looked at me quizzically and signed, "What are you doing?"

A little frantic but holding it together, I said, "My father is here. You have to hide."

Her face fell. I crossed to the bed in two huge strides and pulled her to my chest. I could feel her heart pounding beneath her breastbone.

"Son," he hollered from outside the door. "Open up this instant."

Trying to sound groggy, I called out, "Dad?" Then, I leaned back and looked Molly in the eye. "I have a plan," I signed even though I didn't. "I will fix this. I promise." Her eyes were already rimmed in red, and she did not look convinced.

"What the fuck are you doing in there?" my father hollered.

As I said, "Jesus, Dad. Give me a minute. I was sleeping," I pulled Molly up and ushered her toward the closet. It broke my heart to look at her standing naked in the door frame, my color-coordinated shirts hanging behind her.

"I don't have time to explain, but this will never happen again. I promise."

She shook her head back and forth, and one tear slipped out, carving a path down her cheek.

"Please," I begged her with my hands. "Don't cry, Mol."

She wiped her face and then crouched down on the floor, pulling her knees against her naked chest, toying with the hair on the crown of her head.

I lowered myself down too. Behind me, my father's annoyance raged, "Zackary Worthington, open this fucking door right now!"

"I love you," I signed right before I shut her in.

CHAPTER TWENTY-FOUR

MOLLY

THROUGH THE SLATS in the closet door, I could see their feet and calves. I didn't dare move a muscle. I tried not to even take a heavy breath. I knew that any movement, any at all, could mean sound, and sound would give me away. I wasn't worried about being quiet for Zack. I was still and quiet for me. I didn't want to be the naked girl in the closet who fell in love with a boy who couldn't see that even one minute in the closet the morning after you first made love was too many minutes.

So, I made like a statue. I pretended I was stone. Stone skin, stone lips, stone lungs, stone heart. I pictured all the bits and pieces of myself as cold, smooth marble. Unflinching and unfeeling. Marble didn't shake. It didn't breathe. It didn't cry. Marble didn't feel anything at all. It was just rock.

Eventually, they left. I was sure they were gone. I couldn't see their feet moving any longer, and Zack flicked the lights on and off twice when they departed. A signal especially for me. Still, I remained on the floor in the tiny dark space for a few minutes, pushing away the stillness and the stoicism. I wasn't made of stone. I was a person with fucking feelings, and he hurt me.

I hugged my knees to my breasts, and I cried. I cried because I loved him. I cried because he loved me. And I cried because I knew from the first moment I laid eyes on him that there was no way we could work. I could never be told to hide again. This was the last straw. I took one last deep breath of him, letting the scent of his clothes and all his things flood my nostrils, before I stood, picked up my things and opened the closet door.

The room was much as it was when he put me in the closet, but I was different. I felt like a shadow of myself. My insides were raw and burnt, scorched. Zack Worthington was leaving a brutal scar, one I suspected I would carry forever. I put on my clothes. Blew my nose with a tissue from a box on the desk and took a bottle of water from the tiny fridge in the corner. I was just putting my phone in my purse when the lights overhead flickered.

I turned to the door, hoping to see him standing there, while praying he wasn't. I didn't think I was strong enough to stand my ground and get away from him if I had to see him right then. But it wasn't him. It was just an arm, poking through the door, flashing the lights.

The door pushed open, and the arm turned into Vos, standing inside the room with his eyes covered by his hand. He was holding a piece of white paper that he'd written on with a Sharpie, *Are you decent?*

Using my text-to-voice app, I said, "I am decent, but I'm wondering how you thought I was going to answer you, Vos?"

Opening his eyes, he spoke, and then he smacked his forehead and started laughing.

I rolled my eyes as he pointed at my phone, silently asking if I could pass it to him so he could talk to me.

Before handing it to him, I typed, "You're an idiot right now."

Vos read the words, and then he typed, "Totally. I'm usually an idiot, but I'm smart enough to know this situation sucks. Are you okay?"

I shrugged, and then my brow pinched together as I attempted not to cry.

"He's stupid, Molly. He's crazy about you. I've never seen him like this. I know he thinks he's protecting you, but it can't feel good."

I shrugged again, and, taking the phone back, I typed, "I just want to go home."

Vos nodded and then responded, "I called Cora; she's on her way. She said to tell you that if you want out of here ASAP, you can trust me to walk you to the quad, despite my creeper move with her hair last night."

I looked up from the screen, and Vos was making a face like he was disgusted. He grabbed the phone back and typed, "What the fuck was that, btw? Ew. So embarrassing."

I didn't know how it happened, but I laughed.

Again, Vos grabbed my phone, typed, and then handed it back to me. "I am going to have to learn to sign. I have too many things to say to type to you all the time. You will never get a word in edgewise. Will you teach me?"

I nodded, but I didn't really mean it. If he wanted to speak to me, then he should hire an ASL tutor. Hearing people always asked Deaf people to teach them ASL, even though they would never make friends with a foreigner and assume the foreigner would teach them their language, but somehow, they thought it was a Deaf person's responsibility to make communicating easier for them. Still, I knew Vos was trying to be friendly, and I was too emotionally exhausted to gently point out his privilege, so I let it lie.

Kindly, Vos looped his arm through mine and tilted his head to the door, an invitation to leave. By the time we got downstairs to the bottom floor, I was relieved he escorted me through the frat house. Unlike the night before, the house was crawling with dudes. Most of them were eyeing Vos, sizing up his connection to me, and when we got to the foyer, one guy said something. Vos stopped, snapped angrily at the bully, and then gave him the finger. I guessed the hand gesture was mostly for my benefit.

Once outside, we walked side by side silently, until Cora came running up. She was out of breath and red-faced. She quickly thanked Vos, and then she threw her arms around me, squeezing so tight that I felt my lungs struggle for air, but I didn't care. I was just so happy to see her, to be back in the arms of someone who truly deserved my trust.

CHAPTER TWENTY-FIVE

ZACK

A DELIGHTFUL SURPRISE, that's what my father called his Saturday morning visit. Only there was nothing delightful about it. My father liked to show up unannounced. He did it to me. He did it to my mother. He did it to his employees and his rivals. I'd lived my whole life under the threat that he was just around the next corner, waiting to catch me making a mistake or presenting as less than perfect. He was never without an intention, a logical reason for his sudden appearance.

He said he was in town to manage the final details of a little soiree he was throwing a few weeks later for reunion weekend, which he was, because like all good liars and manipulators, my father relied on truths to make his behaviors seem harmless. When I was younger, he made me feel like I'd imagined his need to control me and check up on me. Now I knew better. I was a commodity to be managed, always. Since I returned from spring break, I'd been avoiding his calls, so he sat across from me to remind me that there were rules to follow. I had his image to uphold.

"You know how these things are," he said, sitting across a white tablecloth from me and cutting into the NY strip on his plate. "Don't trust someone to do what you can manage better."

"You could have had Stephanie call me," I suggested. Stephanie was his assistant "I would have dealt with any issues for you."

"Oh," he scolded, "do you get Stephanie's phone calls? I wasn't sure your phone was working."

He hated excuses, but I gave him one anyway. "It's an intense part of the semester, and I've been busy planning for alumni weekend."

"Yes, of course, and there is also your sleep schedule that keeps you in bed till noon. Right?" To a passerby, he sounded like he was teasing me, but his words were absolutely aggressive.

Normally, as he subtly scolded me, I would have felt small and inadequate, but in that moment, I didn't give a shit that he was pissed. In fact, the last person I wanted to be was his son. All I could think about was Molly. When he and I sat down, I tucked my phone under the table and sent Molly a text, but she hadn't responded. It just said, *I meant it. I love you.*

I kept picturing her, tiny and fetal, in my closet. It was wrong. It shouldn't have happened. I'd been trying to walk a tightrope but threw her off like dead weight so I could stay balanced. *Fuck. Fuck.* I had to go back. I had to fix it.

My father continued to focus on his agenda. "Have you found a date for the weekend, preferably someone blonde, maybe from the South? My polling in with conservative women could be better."

"No," I said curtly.

"No blondes or no southern belles?" he chided. Again, it sounded like he was teasing me, but he was pushing.

I couldn't listen to his controlling manipulative nonsense. I needed to get back to Molly. To the average person, it might not have felt like a rebellion, but when I stood, I broke one of my father's unspoken rules: *When he was speaking, I should be listening.*

"What are you doing?" my father snapped, pausing the movement of his knife and fork.

"I have somewhere else I have to be," I spoke sternly.

"Sit down," he commanded.

I pushed in my chair, grabbed my coat, and tried to act civilized. "Let me know if you need my help making sure your reunion event goes smoothly."

My father's voice was eerily calm when he said, "You seem agitated, son. Are you agitated?"

"No, sir. Just …" I trailed off, unwilling to offer another explanation.

Poking his fork into his steak, he sawed at the meat with his knife and said, "I am curious what is so important that you would want to rush off so quickly."

A veiled threat. He probably didn't know about Molly, but he was warning me that he knew I was hiding something, and if I continued to defy him, he would make the effort to unearth my secrets. I pulled my chair out and sat down again. If I wanted to protect Molly from the judgment and cruelty that was my father, then I needed to stay.

As soon as my father was gone, I texted, but Molly still didn't answer. I tried sleeping on her doorstep again, but she never came home. I called Cora, but it went straight to voicemail. I appealed to Vos, asking him to approach her or Cora for me, but he said, "I love you, man, but I think you're on your own this time."

The thing was, I understood why she shut me out. I deserved it. There was no miscommunication. I literally hid her in a closet. It wasn't a metaphor; my love was in the closet.

I took a woman who spent her whole life fighting to convince the world she deserved to be heard and seen, and I intentionally hid her. Just to add insult to injury, when did I push her into the closet? Why, the morning after we made love for the first time. I had always prided myself on my ability to examine and manage situations, but when it came to Molly, I was a fool time and again. I promised her I would do better, and as soon as I was put to the test, I caved. It didn't matter that I intended to do differently. It mattered that I failed to stand tall when I needed to.

I should have stayed away. She was better off without me, but I couldn't stop myself. I was withering without her. Food had no flavor. Sleep was impossible. I didn't care if I showered or studied. I didn't care what nonsense my idiot brothers got up to. I just wanted her forgiveness. I just wanted to feel her skin, hold her in my arms, watch her sleep. I was crazed, shredded on the inside.

At the very least, I needed to talk to her one more time. Let her see how losing her affected me. At my wits' end, I devised a stupid plan. I cleaned myself up, marched down to the administration building and charmed a registrar out of her schedule. Then, like a maniac, I waited outside Dr. Clark's Intro to Psychology class, prepared to ambush her.

When the class was over, the students funneled out. I scanned them all. Not her, not her, not her. Some were laughing and talking. Others were carrying books or looking at their phones. Their departure felt like a rhythmic dance: a couple of speedy staccato early birds, a moderato clump of chatty Cathys, followed by distracted legato slowpokes who seemed to move through thicker air than the rest of us.

I had all but given up hope when Molly came through the door. She was preceded by a young woman who must have been her interpreter because they stopped just through the threshold and signed their goodbyes. The woman was older, in her thirties. She hugged Molly casually and turned to walk away but then slowed and turned back, pulling Molly into a tight embrace.

Crushed in the hug, Molly's face was forced my way. She looked pale, ghastly really. Her eyes were closed, but there was something sunken about them. And she looked thin, too thin. It was clear she was suffering too.

The woman released her, leaning back to sign, "You will be okay. Heartbreak is terrible, but we survive it."

Molly nodded anxiously, and her jaw tightened as she worked to hold back her tears. Suddenly, it didn't matter that I was suffering. It mattered that Molly stopped suffering. I could have run to her, dropped to my knees and begged her forgiveness. Maybe she would have forgiven me or settled for the man before her just to escape the pain she was feeling. But as it stood, I couldn't guarantee her suffering would end.

Molly needed someone brave and real, like her. She needed someone who would put her feelings front and center. Someone who didn't act based on his own selfish needs. I wasn't certain I could be that man, but ambushing her when I hurt her, and she clearly didn't want to see me wasn't a good start.

I was terrified her interpreter was right. Maybe if I wasted too much time, Molly would forget me. Or maybe she would meet someone better, someone who was already together enough to deserve her. But it didn't matter; I had to take that chance because, if I wanted Molly back, I needed to first be the man she deserved, not a hero or a villain – an honest to goodness man, one who lived his truth and was willing to muck about, flaws and all.

For Molly but also for myself, it was time to crawl out from my father's shadow, to stop taking the path of least resistance and boldly be me. Molly was right—being human was messy. I was an asshole, but I was also kind. I was a geek and a preppy frat boy. I was a man, not a boy, and my father's choices for me could no longer rule my life. Being wholly me was my only way back to Molly. I just had to buckle down and figure out how to get there.

Less than a week later, I was in a suit, standing at a high-top table, nursing a glass of wine as my father worked the room at the alumni reunion event he planned. He was already annoyed with me because I'd defied him and arrived single. He hosted an alumni event so he could make sure he spent time with the people he considered most important and in the know. He demanded my attendance because my role as president of his fraternity strengthened his connection to all the brothers, new and old. And I was guessing that a pretty girl on my arm would have given him something to say about me that shone. He wasn't interested in me shining on my own. I was just fodder for his engaging chitchat. Since I was a child, his general policy was that I was there to be seen but not heard.

It was not my intention to declare my independence from my father in the middle of his event. I hadn't really made a plan yet. It had only been a handful of days since I realized I couldn't beg for Molly's forgiveness without claiming the right to be my own person. I wasn't sure what that would look like, and so far the only thing I accomplished was marching into Vos's room with a copy of the *Dune* board game that I ordered on Amazon and announcing I wanted to play.

Anyway, I was standing at the high-top doing nothing special, when none other than Kaitlyn Parker walked over with her husband, Martin Sandeke. Beyond their alumni status, it was obvious to me why my father invited them. Martin was a man with deep pockets, and my father loved deep pockets. That said, I would bet my left nut that Sandeke wouldn't want anything to do with my dad. Martin was a man of honor. A man who looked to make the world a better place. But who was I to say?

Kaitlyn was somewhat joyful about running into me. "Oh my god, Zack, I sound like someone's grandma, but I cannot believe that you're like a full-grown man!"

As was appropriate, I responded with a little chuckle, but then I said, "Debatable," which felt way too telling. Definitely not my usual couth, but instead of feeling terrified that I was offering her a hint of my truth, I felt liberated. So, I added, "I've had a complicated semester. Just sort of trying to work out who the adult version of Zack Worthington is, ya know?"

Kaitlyn stared at me for a beat, her eyes blinking, once, twice, and then she grinned, revealing the gap in her front teeth. Leaning in and lowering her voice to something akin to a whisper but not quite so subtle, she said, "Man, I'm gonna be honest with you, I'm still trying to figure out who the adult version of Kaitlyn Parker is."

Martin shot her an adoring look while shaking his head. "The woman basically plays every instrument invented, and still she is never satisfied."

"Self-confidence is perhaps overrated," I snarked, feeling completely welcome and comfortable being myself among them.

Kaitlyn laughed and poked Martin in the side, noting, "If it is, this guy didn't get the message."

Hungry to relay more truth bombs, I was about to ask them their favorite movie, when my father appeared, draping his arm over my shoulder. "I hope my offspring isn't talking your ear off with some nonsense," he chided.

Instinctually, I chewed the inside of my cheek, a physical manifestation of the anxiety I felt when my father subtly put me down to silence me.

"Not at all," Martin said icily, clearly not appreciating my father at all.

Sandeke's tone was not lost on my father. His smile widened, but I saw the vein in his forehead pulse as he switched gears and addressed Kaitlyn. "Sweetheart, I really am so happy to see you. How are you doing—with your music, correct?"

All the whimsy and camaraderie she had thrown in my direction was absent from her response to my dad. Suddenly, she seemed poised but uninterested. "Well. Thank you."

"Quite well," Martin added. "She's the composer for a chart-topping band; perhaps you've heard of them—Redburn?"

"Of course, a true feat," my father commended in a general sense, leaving his knowledge of Redburn, or lack thereof, up for debate.

"And a constant source of frustration," Kaitlyn admitted. "This week we are struggling to find a drummer worth our time. Ours broke his wrist, and we need someone to fill in while he's recovering."

My guts rolled at the words that fell from her lips. "Really?" I asked incredulously, not quite able to believe Mol's luck.

Surprised by my response, Kaitlyn furrowed her brow at me and quirked her chin. "Does that surprise you? I feel like a band needing a musician is kinda par for the course."

I could feel myself grinning. "No. Shit, don't mind me. It's just that the world works in such mysterious ways. I happen to know an incredible, passionate and unusually talented drummer."

Kaitlyn grinned back at me. "Really?"

"Totally. She's a student in the music…"

"Son," my father interrupted me, "please don't bother these people by suggesting they should hire some immature friend of yours."

He had no idea he was dismissing Molly. But his ignorance didn't matter. Just the fact that he suggested someone should ignore her was the match to my fire. My father could go fuck himself.

Turning my face to him, I calmly said, "Could you stuff your bullshit for five minutes? You don't know anything about the woman I am discussing. You have no idea if she is talented or not. You only assume she isn't because you think no one but you is intelligent enough to understand anything. And I'm so over it."

My father grabbed my shoulder, turning his body so I was closer to him, and then dropped his tone to a whispered snarl, "You are certainly proving that you are not intelligent enough to understand anything." He tried to hand me his empty wine glass. "Why don't you make yourself useful and refill my drink?"

"NO," I snapped, the word vibrating the space between us. "For once, you will not interrupt me or render me invisible. I'm going to talk to these people, and if you don't like it, too fucking bad. You really want to stop me, Dad? You want us to have a showy brawl, right here in the middle of your event?"

His nostrils flared, but the threat of a scene silenced him for the moment.

Turning back to Kaitlyn and Martin, I was completely composed and calm when I said, "I'm sorry. I didn't mean to air the dumpster fire that is my father's nature in front of you two, but there is no way I am going to let you miss out on the drummer I'm telling you about. Her name is Molly Mills, and she's incredible."

CHAPTER TWENTY-SIX

MOLLY

I ALMOST CALLED in sick for the alumni gig. I couldn't imagine I had the energy to play. I wasn't getting enough sleep, and I'd been surviving on junk food for the last few weeks. Honestly, I hadn't even eaten a whole lot of that. Anything I ate seemed to make the hole in my core feel deeper.

Sometimes I wondered if I was going to drown in my heartbreak. How could one person I'd only known for a handful of months become so important? How could he have gotten under my skin so quickly? It was like walking through fog all the time, like being lost in a dampening haze, knowing there was something somewhere—something so much better, but I had no way to get there. My days didn't feel real because I couldn't discuss them with him. It was flabbergasting.

More than once since the morning he tucked me in his closet, I found myself looking in the mirror and thinking, *You knew better. It was doomed from the start, and you did it anyway.* I blamed myself.

For the first couple of weeks, he tried to reach me, but I wasn't strong enough to talk to him. I would give in to his apologies, just like I had the time before. I wanted him, and he wanted me, but our desire didn't mean we made sense. We were worlds apart. Total opposites. One punk rock, one preppy. One Deaf, one hearing. One fighting for acceptance, one conforming for it. There were too many bridges to build. I wasn't strong enough to fight for us both.

Still, late at night, tossing and turning in the darkness of my dorm room, I stopped trying to shake free from the haunting of my heartbreak, and I'd remember the moments. The honesty and silliness in his text messages. The awkwardness of his clandestine romp between the trees on the quad. His altering of the movie theater policy to include me. The giddy excitement he felt discovering a *Dune* game existed. The intoxicating magic of making love with him and the ferocious snarl I elicited when I told him to fuck me. Alone in my bed, I would forgive my choice, knowing I couldn't have stopped it if I tried. Even if it was doomed from the start, there was no world where I would erase knowing him. It was like my mother said: the grief was worth it. Even if I had to walk through the fog of living without him forever.

Each day I got up and tried to adjust. I tried to carry on and manage my new normal. I tried to live in the reality of being myself without him. My need to continue to exist, to refind reality after my connection to Zack was why I decided not to bow out of the alumni gig. Before him, I was a drummer. Drumming was the engine that drove my train, so I knew it was best to refocus my energy on that passion.

At my most dapper and absolutely loaded with caffeine, I took the stage with the band from my rock and roll performance class. We were back in the Keller Theater, only this time it was set up like a wedding, complete with cocktail tables and flower arrangements. We played an entire set in front of an empty dance floor to a milling crowd of chattering faces and passing trays loaded with specialty blue university-themed cocktails. But the lack of investment from our audience didn't bother me. For me, playing the drums was never about being seen or even about being heard. It was about connecting to the rhythm, my conduit to some kind of universal consciousness. So as soon as the first vibration licked the soles of my feet, I felt relief.

I clung to my sticks like they were my lifeline. Pounding out my rhythms, I let go for the first time in weeks. My mind cleared, making way for the groove, and beyond that there was nothing else. With each repeated phrase, I felt freer, like I could draw breaths without my heart clenching.

I knew it wasn't permanent. I knew that when the rhythm stopped, my heart would still be in pieces, but I had my sticks. I could and would always play the drums. I was still the woman brazen and bold enough to chase her unconventional dream, the woman who deserved to get noticed as a drummer because she was talented, and also the woman who quite simply was lucky to have a passion she could access so easily, even if it never made me a dollar. I was a drummer, and no one could take that away from me.

When we were done, I stayed seated on my drum throne, sticks still in hand, and let the adrenaline course through my body. The vibrations rumbling my joints reminded me of Zack, the feeling of his touch, the way it shook me to the core, but I didn't let it sour. I pushed past the thought, tagged it as lovely and returned to the high of being good at the thing I loved.

In my back pocket, my telephone buzzed. It was either Cora, who had most definitely snuck her way into the room, or maybe Joey or one of the other band members, but either way, it could wait a minute. Three more deep breaths. Three more moments of clarity.

Very few people were paying attention to our existence. The other members of our makeshift band were unplugging their instruments, making room for whoever was playing after us. But then, Dr. Williams, my professor, appeared, shuffling out from the wings of the stage. He was approaching me with a woman. My brain did that thing where it raced, trying to figure out how I knew her.

He was holding a pad and pencil, and once they were directly in front of me, I stood. Still barefoot, I watched the letters he was writing appear upside down, "Ms. Mills, I'd like to introduce you to Kaitlyn Parker."

***

My mouth was dry, and I couldn't figure out whether to cross or uncross my legs. Cora and I were sitting at a fancy cocktail table waiting for Kaitlyn to return from the bathroom.

With wide eyes and an unsettled stomach, I turned to Cora and signed, "Did Kaitlyn Parker just FaceTime Abram Fletcher while I was playing?"

Cora, looking as stunned as I felt, smiled and nodded.

"Did she then approach me and tell me I was the most talented drummer she's seen play in a long time?"

Cora nodded again, her knees starting to bounce.

"Did she say she wanted to pay for me to come stay in New York, including any accommodations I needed, and offer me a gig playing for Redburn?"

Cora's head bobbed up and down at a speed that seemed insane, and then she threw her arms around me and crushed me to her chest. When she released me, she was clapping her hands together and grinning like a fool.

Her love for me was so big that her response to my good fortune looked like she'd won the lottery, but I was more nervous and confused than anything else. I knew Kaitlyn was an alum. She mentioned that immediately. And she told us they had been looking for a drummer for Redburn's new album for weeks to no avail.

Cora had interpreted her words when she said, "We've seen technically talented drummers, but the magic was missing. I can see you have it. When you were up there playing, it rolled off you like waves. It's about the music for you, not the money or the fame, just the music."

I was certain she believed those words. There was nothing contrived or saccharin in her expression, but I also remembered Zack mentioning he knew her, and I was totally unsettled about the possibility of Zack bringing me this luck. I couldn't possibly agree to take the job until I was one hundred percent sure it was a genuine offer. So, while Cora celebrated, I racked my brain trying to figure out the least offensive way to ask if he was involved in bringing her into my world.

Annoyed by my lack of enthusiasm, Cora lifted her eyebrows and stuck out her chin as she signed, "Why are you not happy right now? You should be over the moon."

Struggling with my own thoughts, I offered, "A few weeks ago, Zack told me he knew her."

"So?"

"What if he made this happen?" I moved my hands slowly, trying to decide how I felt about what I was saying.

Cora grew still and heaved out a heavy breath. She squeezed my shoulder before she signed, "Then you should thank him."

I understood what she was saying. As far as Cora was concerned, it didn't matter how Kaitlyn came to hear me play. What mattered was that she saw my talent and wanted to employ it. But was it really that simple? What if Zack was using Kaitlyn as a way to get back into my good graces?

"Doesn't it just seem too good to be true?" I asked.

Suddenly, Cora's cheeks rouged, and her brow furrowed. Fiery, she whipped her hands about when she said, "Don't do this. My brother does what you're doing right now, and I hate it. When something good happens to you, don't let the way the world overlooks you because you're different become the foundation of your self-worth. If Zack turned her on to you, it's because you're amazing. It's because he knows you're amazing. Kaitlyn Parker isn't going to hire you as some ploy. She wants you because you're the best she's seen. She told you that. Believe it. Let the good thing happen."

Behind Cora, I watched Kaitlyn move through the crowd confidently, pausing to touch the arm and kiss the cheek of a tall, handsome man whom I assumed was her husband before returning to the table with Cora and me. I knew Cora was right, but I just had to know. Awkwardly I grabbed the glass of water in front of me and took a huge swig before signing, "What made you come to this event today?"

Cora rolled her eyes, but out of respect for me, she interpreted my words exactly.

Kaitlyn smiled and leaned back in her chair before she said, "Zack asked that I didn't mention his name, but I was clear with him that if you asked anything, anything at all about how I found you, I was going to be honest. I don't do drama. So, let me clarify immediately, my profession isn't a game. I ran into him yesterday and happened to mention that I was struggling to find a drummer…"

I thought I finished the story by adding, "And he suggested you see me play."

"Yes." She nodded, and then a delighted impish look crossed her face as she noted, "Despite his father's ire, he did. He told me you were the talent I needed and where I could find you, but that is where his involvement begins and ends."

Next to me, Cora's jaw dropped. Kaitlyn had no idea how much she revealed, or how thankful I was to hear her words, but Cora knew what it meant for Zack to speak of me in front of his father.

Completely uncharacteristically, an emotionally overcome Cora started blubbering words and forgot to sign them for me. Kaitlyn was laughing as Cora was pulling me from my chair.

"What are you doing?" I signed, holding my ground and not letting her pull me from my chair.

Realizing she was flustered, Cora regained her ability to sign. "You should go. You should go to him."

I wasn't sure. I wanted to. I wanted to believe that standing up to his father for me was Zack being the man I always thought he could be. The man who shuffled off the pretense and lived his own life, chasing the things that made him happy. But even if he did that, we'd still come from two different worlds. He'd still be hearing, and I'd still be Deaf.

Cora argued for him, "He doesn't have to be perfect, Mol. I've never had a man look at me the way that man looks at you, and he fucked up for sure, but people do that. And then we learn to be better, bigger people."

"Can we discuss this later?" I glanced uncomfortably at Kaitlyn. I did not want to have this conversation in front of her. Cora wasn't speaking her words, but even if we were silent, it was clear she was upset, and it felt rude.

There was no stopping Cora. She angrily snapped her thumb and first two fingers together, like a monster clamping its mouth shut. "No."

"We're too different," I offered.

I could almost see the smoke coming out of her ears when she asked, "Because he can hear?"

I nodded yes.

"I don't know if you know this," she snapped, "but I can hear every sound in the world, and you let me love you."

"It's not the same," I signed emphatically. "You get me. You get my world, my culture. You know better."

"You're right. I do," Cora signed smartly. "I learned to know better – for love."

I just stared at her. Her words were like a slap—they stung, but they also clanged into a wall in my brain that I didn't know was there. I was afraid. I was afraid of Zack. I was afraid that he would always hurt me. And maybe he would, but the only person hurting me right now was me. I was hiding from him. I was pretending there was nothing to discuss. I was making the assumption that our love wouldn't work. We'd switched places. He was out there trying to be brave, and I was still hiding in the closet.

"I need to go to him," I signed to Cora.

Cora laughed, her eyes welling with tears, and then her attention turned to Kaitlyn, who must have said something.

Still looking away, Cora interpreted, "He loves her?"

Cora nodded yes.

"She loves him?"

Cora nodded yes again.

"She should go to him."

Cora shrugged, like *duh*. "That's what I'm saying."

"Don't let her worry about me. I'll chase her down if I have to. I want her in our band."

I looked from Cora's hand to Kaitlyn's face.

She scrunched her nose and nodded a hard yes, and, then, grinning at me, she held up her pinkie, offering me a promise. She was awesome. I wanted to cry. I felt the happy sappy tears sneaking up my throat as I wrapped my pinkie around hers, and we shook on it.

Then, she pointed at the door and mouthed, "Go."

CHAPTER TWENTY-SEVEN

ZACK

I WAS TRAPPED at yet another alumni event, at my frat house this time. I stood at the far edge of the back yard, nursing a seltzer, watching the crowd mill in and out of the back door. My father was on the patio, glaring at me from time to time. I hadn't spoken to him since I put him in his place earlier in the weekend. My father, on the other hand, had left me a plethora of scathing, angry, hateful messages, but much to my surprise, I hadn't been kicked out of school or disowned. All my credit cards still worked, and my car wasn't towed away.

I kept waiting for him to implode, glancing over my shoulder expecting goons or cops or something sinister, but there was just his nasty death stare. I'd spent my life terrified of him. Terrified that he would ruin me and anyone I cared about because he implied he would, but so far, he wasn't actually an evil villain like Thanos. He was just an angry asshole, a blowhard.

I hoped Kaitlyn would call after she saw Molly play, so I kept checking my phone, but nothing. Six months ago, I would have been all about making sure this event was absolutely perfect, but honestly, why? If my brothers were going to make a mess of things, then so be it. That was their prerogative. I would survive. Maybe they needed to fall on their faces, or maybe they didn't need me to stay upright. Maybe my belief that they'd fall apart without me was like my dad's threats—not really real. Either way, they seemed to be doing just fine, socializing with the men who had inhabited this house for decades before them. They'd donned their navy blue sport coats and their khakis, and appeared to be perfectly happy to eat tiny salmon and shrimp salad sandwiches and drink Chablis.

I watched them with their older, tidier counterparts and wondered if the alumni were pretending they didn't know that the fridge in the kitchen was filled with beer and the pantry with Easy Cheese, or if they were wishing they could return to being the younger more unruly versions of themselves. I snickered to myself picturing the herd of older dudes—led by my father—descending on our kitchen like a wild and violent raiding party and then holding the aerosol cans above their mouths as they unloaded the neon orange slime into their throats.

"Why are you smiling?" Vos approached from my left and then added, "I thought the Zack-who-smiled phase of your life went out the door with the unmentionable pretty pixie."

I felt the sadness rise up and drop the corners of my lips, but I said, "You can mention her."

"Can I?" he asked, curious. "Because I feel like over the last week you just gave up, like you stopped fighting for her all together."

I shook my head. "No. I'm trying to fight for her. But I can't beg her forgiveness if I can't do better. I need to be the man she deserves."

Vos shook his head and sighed. "Not that my opinion matters…"

I interrupted him, "Of course it does. You're my best friend. Your opinion always matters."

Vos looked away for a second, clearly taken aback by my declaration of friendship, and then he made a show of standing tall. "Well then, I was going to say you're good enough already – but not because you won't make mistakes again. You're never gonna be able to promise her that, Zack. You won't make this mistake again, but you'll make others. She might not forgive you. But you let her cool down. Now, find a way to get through. Because I think you love her, and when you love someone, you don't just let them walk away."

"Maybe," I said, still unsure. "I'll think about it."

"Fair."

I checked my phone again. Still nothing.

"Are you waiting on something?" Vos asked.

Looking up, I started to answer him, but then I noticed Molly. She was standing at the back door. At first I wasn't certain she was real. Her hair was loose, and she was all dressed up and looking fancy. I blinked a few times, thinking that if she was a mirage, she'd disappear. But she didn't. She stepped over the threshold of the slider into the grass and scanned the space, looking for someone, looking for me. Molly was looking for me.

I took a step out of the shadow of the trees, and she smiled immediately when she saw me. She fucking smiled, a stupid ear-to-ear smile that made my stomach flip. From where she stood, she signed, "We need to talk."

She was happy. I could see it all over her face. That meant Kaitlyn loved her. And maybe Vos was right. Maybe I'd already found my way to get through.

I grinned back at her and asked, "Are you a professional drummer right now?"

She nodded.

"Fuck yeah you are."

Next to me Vos grumbled, "I have to learn to sign. It's like fucking torture."

She and I started moving, pulled like magnets toward each other. There was some shifting through people, but I kept her in my sights. She loved me. I wasn't sure what changed, and I hadn't meant to do it, but I could see it. I could see that the anger and sadness were gone. Molly came to me. She was here to tell me she wanted me.

When I was about six feet from her, I tried to shift around an alumnus and got caught up in a shuffle that made us break eye contact, and when I looked for her gaze again, she was hidden behind the torso of a man I knew too well: my father.

I could hear him speaking, "You must be lost. This is a private event." His tone was hoity and elitist, and I wondered if more people thought he was an asshole than either he or I realized. "It would be best if you would kindly make your way to the door."

Coming up behind him, I laid my hand on his shoulder and pulled gently to get his attention. My gesture had the intended effect. He turned toward me. I signed as I spoke, "Molly can't hear you, Dad."

My father's nostrils flared, and a little too loudly, he said, "Well then, perhaps you can tell her that she shouldn't be here now."

I thought we would fight. Like when I pictured the moment, when I finally put my foot down and told my father I wasn't going to be his boy anymore, I thought there would be a nasty brawl of epic proportion. I pictured a dramatic scenario—a movie-worthy battle with screaming and yelling and maybe even violence. But when the moment arrived, I wasn't a beast or a character in a dramatic scene. Suddenly, I was a man, a kind and gentle one, who had finally figured out how to love a woman who was absolutely more than I deserved.

I didn't need to snarl or throw a punch. I didn't need to be an animal. I just needed to tell him that he'd lost control of me, and there was nothing he could do about it because I didn't care what he thought at all. If she were mine, he couldn't hurt me.

So I simply said, "Actually, she can be here whenever she wants. She is always welcome where I am." Then, I took a step forward and turned so I was standing next to her, tentatively reaching my fingers toward hers, fluttering my pinky against hers. When she welcomed my tiny touch, I went full boar and took her hand in mine.

People started to stare. The necks craned to see why Senator Worthington and his son seemed tense. My father's jaw tightened, and his brow furrowed. "Son, this party is for invited guests only."

"No problem, Dad." I stayed calm. "We can leave."

From across the lawn, Vos started moving toward us and called out, "I think it's fine if Molly stays, Senator." He moved quickly, and before I knew it, he was standing on Molly's other side. The chatter around us seemed to go silent.

My father's eyes narrowed. He went to speak, but before he said anything, Dickie stepped around him, taking the space next to me as he said, "Yeah, me too. If the Prez says she stays, she stays, sir."

And then like dominos, my brothers were all around us. They stood with me. I was their leader, and they stood with me.

Molly squeezed my hand. I turned and looked into her welling gaze. She knew what it meant. She knew I thought I was alone, and it turned out I never was.

Molly signed, "I love you."

And in the immortal words of Han Solo, I replied, "I know."

It took her a second, but then she laughed.

CHAPTER TWENTY-EIGHT

MOLLY

Late Summer

WAKING up in a hotel room still felt foreign. The sheets and pillows were plush, and the air was cool, but time and space seemed to disappear behind the blackout shades. Despite an entire summer of bouncing from one hotel to the next, the moments before my consciousness was totally aware felt disconcerting. Nothing smelled familiar. And then, the heavy arm of the world's worst interpreter tightened around my middle, and I remembered that my life had gone from normal to out of this world in a matter of months.

If someone asked me to conjure up a picture of my perfect life, I was living it. Kaitlyn and Abram hired me to help finish up the most recent Redburn album with them and to join Redburn on the road for their summer tour while their regular drummer nursed his broken wrist. It was a temporary gig, but I did not go unnoticed. I already had a couple offers on the table to join other bands as a substitute drummer, and I'd been approached by a Broadway director who needed a percussionist for a rock and roll musical.

As if being a professional drummer wasn't enough—whatever was flopsy and flimsy, lost and ungrounded about Zack had completely evaporated. Sure, he still made mistakes attempting to interpret for me, but after thwarting his dad by taking my hand that afternoon on the frat house lawn, Zack blossomed, where blossoming was defined by the consumption of nerdy sci-fi/fantasy memorabilia. He was like a new man, the preppiest, sexiest nerd in the entire world.

Senator Worthington no longer had any say in the matter of Zack's future. Despite how he'd made Zack fear him, the senator was very concerned with looking like a consummate family man and a good, supportive father. It turned out that cutting off his obviously successful son didn't fit well with that image. So, while he wasn't happy with Zack's choices, particularly the decision to spend the summer on the road with Redburn and me, the senator was more bluster than action.

Zack was definitely still struggling to understand how that was possible. Sometimes he would just stare off into space for a while, and then he would look at me and sign something like, "How did he convince me that he ruled the world?"

I didn't like the senator at all. He was a nasty man who emotionally manipulated his son for years. The mere thought of him made me want to snarl, but there were no real answers for Zack. His father hurt him, and I wasn't sure there was a way to heal that, other than time and therapy. So, when he asked, it was probably a rhetorical question, but I always signed something like, "He's a total douche canoe?"

I hoped I might make him laugh and remind him that we were happy.

We were happy.

We were in love.

So even when waking up in a hotel room felt odd, waking up next to Zack felt like heaven. We were spoons, all night long. I didn't know how he did it, but every morning he seemed to know I was awake before I even opened my eyes, and today was no different. He dragged the tip of his pinkie, pointer finger and thumb up the outside of my thigh. Running his *I love you* up my thigh was a sign that we developed together—a sexy shorthand for *good morning, I love you.*

When we woke, he was always hard. There were a lot of days over the summer when we didn't have time to enjoy each other, but this hotel room was the last stop. The tour ended the night before. So, we had nowhere to be but with each other.

I pushed my tush back, pressing into him, and felt the warm stutter of his gasp against the nape of my neck. The hand around my waist slipped down past my belly button, sliding under the hem of my panties. His touch was languid and light, a flutter. He loved to tease me. He loved to slowly tantalize me until I was shivering in his hands. He also liked to come deep inside me, so I went on the Pill because I liked that too. That was how we came that morning in the hotel after my last Redburn show. We stayed curled together, still spoons as he entered me from behind, and I clenched around him, panting my release.

Afterwards, Zack reached up and pulled the little chain on the lamp on the night table, flooding the room with light. Most mornings, Zack made his way to the bathroom in the dark, so I turned to face him, knowing that if he turned on the bedside light, it was because he wanted to talk.

He furrowed his brow and signed, "I'm sort of aimless. I used to know exactly where I was headed, and I hated it. But now my future is mostly this blur, an abyss."

He was sitting like a kid, cross-legged on the bed beside me wearing a black t-shirt that had *rebel scum* printed across the front and a pair of boxers, straight out of Brooks Brothers, pink with little navy flamingos scattered evenly across the fabric. Even though he was clearly trying to have a serious talk, I couldn't help but grin at him. He was somehow both manly and adorkable.

He shook his head at me. "Mol, I'm trying to tell you that my life is utterly unplanned, and that it's completely possible I'll wind up a shiftless loser who spends his days playing video games… and you're grinning at me."

Scrunching my nose, I teasingly waved off his laments and signed, "Video games are fun."

One corner of his mouth lifted in a half smirk. He loved me. He told me all the time, but it was also there in the softness of his eyes. We stared at each other for a minute before he said, "Live with me."

I laughed because I thought he was waxing poetic. "In the frat house? That's not really my scene."

He shook his head. "Me neither. It's so dirty. I've learned to love those guys, I have, but the bathroom in that place is horrendous." He smiled at me before I watched his hands and his lips saying, "Get an apartment with me."

I swallowed, realizing he was serious. Lately my life had been such a whirlwind that I honestly hadn't thought much past the summer.

"You want to leave the fraternity and live with me?"

He nodded. Then he signed, "I want to spend my life with you, Molly. I may not know what I am going to do—but I certainly know who I want to do it all with. It's you, only you. It will always be you."

I tried to maintain my composure as my fingers shaped the "O" and the "K," but my lip trembled, and my eyes welled with tears. I hadn't washed up when I got home after the show, so I wiped at my eyes to keep mascara from running down my face before rolling them at him. "All this lovey-dovey-ness is gonna ruin my rep as an edgy punk pixie."

He laughed at me and teased, "Mol, I own multiple pairs of khaki slacks and at least two shirts with Yoda puns. If I'm your man, your credibility as a hard-core rocker is shot."

"Babe," I signed, crawling into his lap. "Yoda is as hardcore as they come."

"Hardcore, we are," he joked, flipping his sentence like the tiny Jedi master.

"Live together, we will," I quipped back.

And then he kissed me until I started shivering again.

ABOUT THE AUTHOR

Lola West writes short, sweet, smart, silly, sexy romance. With a PhD in women's studies and a flair for the dramatic, Lola likes to keep it real. Her loves are cotton candy, astronomy, kitten heels and small-town hunks. Lola's heroes make you swoon and her heroines talk back. Also, she believes that consent is always sexy, even in books.

You can learn more about Lola by visiting lolawestromance.com and find a **FREE READ** or you can find her hanging out all over the internet.

Find Lola West online:
Follow on: Instagram
Follow on: Facebook
Follow on: Goodreads
Follow on: Bookbub
Follow on: Tiktok
Facebook group: Sugary Sweet & Lots of Heat

Find Smartypants Romance online:
Website: www.smartypantsromance.com
Facebook: www.facebook.com/smartypantsromance/
Goodreads: www.goodreads.com/smartypantsromance
Twitter: @smartypantsrom
Instagram: @smartypantsromance
Newsletter: https://smartypantsromance.com/newsletter/

ALSO BY LOLA WEST

With the Band

Prequel: You Rock

The Maverick

The Killjoy

Spin off: Rock Candy

Big Sky Cowboy Series

Tofu Cowboy

Her Comeback

Imperfect Harmony

Wild Child

Her First Rodeo

Spin off:Mistletoe in Malibu

Love on Island Series

Screw Flirting

Reckless Boy

Rockin' Her Curves

The Christmas Tart

Summer's Dad Bod

Falling for the Opposition

Code of Matrimony by April White (#2.5)

Code of Ethics by April White (#3)

Cipher Office Series

Weight Expectations by M.E. Carter (#1)

Sticking to the Script by Stella Weaver (#2)

Cutie and the Beast by M.E. Carter (#3)

Weights of Wrath by M.E. Carter (#4)

Common Threads Series

Mad About Ewe by Susannah Nix (#1)

Give Love a Chai by Nanxi Wen (#2)

Key Change by Heidi Hutchinson (#3)

Not Since Ewe by Susannah Nix (#4)

Lost Track by Heidi Hutchinson (#5)

Educated Romance

Work For It Series

Street Smart by Aly Stiles (#1)

Heart Smart by Emma Lee Jayne (#2)

Book Smart by Amanda Pennington (#3)

Smart Mouth by Emma Lee Jayne (#4)

Play Smart by Aly Stiles (#5)

Look Smart by Aly Stiles (#6)

Smart Move by Amanda Pennington (#7)

Lessons Learned Series

Under Pressure by Allie Winters (#1)

Not Fooling Anyone by Allie Winters (#2)

Can't Fight It by Allie Winters (#3)

The Vinyl Frontier by Lola West (#4)

Out of this World

www.ingramcontent.com/pod-product-compliance
Lightning Source LLC
Chambersburg PA
CBHW030941210726
48290CB00007B/2279